MW01254652

Tales of Dune

Expanded Edition

International Bestselling Series

TALES OF
DUNE
EXPANDED EDITION

BRIAN HERBERT
and
KEVIN J. ANDERSON

Caezik SF & Fantasy
in partnership with
WordFire Press

This book was originally published by WordFire Press. This edition is published by Caezik SF & Fantasy, an imprint of Arc Manor in partnership with WordFire Press.

Cover painting by Stephen Youll

ISBN: 978-1-64710-069-8

First Caezik/WordFire Edition. First Printing December 2022.
1 2 3 4 5 6 7 8 9 10

An imprint of Arc Manor LLC

www.CaezikSF.com

www.WordFire.com

Contents

The Butlerian Jihad Period

The Dune Period

After the Scattering

Introduction

The Dune universe sprawls across countless planets and dozens of millennia. Frank Herbert's original six Dune novels in addition to the fourteen other books we have added to the canon tell large parts of the story, but sometimes an idea only warrants a briefer exploration.

Considering the immensity of the Dune universe, we often have trouble keeping each novel from getting too big. There are so many potential story lines and intriguing ideas to explore. The wealth of material leaves many side stories that can be told, hors d'oeuvres to accompany the exotic main course.

Sometimes, a short story was exactly what we needed.

Even before the publication of our first new Dune novel, *House Atreides*, we delved into some of the missing pieces in the original classic. When we wrote "A Whisper of Caladan Seas" and published it in *Amazing Stories* in 1999, it was the first piece of new Dune fiction published since the death of Frank Herbert thirteen years earlier. The issue promptly sold out: even back issues are no longer available. And it whet the appetite of Dune fans for the release of the new novel by Bantam Books. *House Atreides* became a runaway bestseller, selling three times the publisher's projections, and proving that Dune fans were alive and well and hungry for more.

As we wrote our novels, we looked for opportunities to write standalone stories, interesting tales that couldn't fit into the larger novels. We wrote character studies, connective stories, side stories, pieces that would fill in the gaps. Some of these stories were published in magazines, in online venues, in anthologies, while others were released as special promotional booklets by our publisher, Tor Books.

Tales of Dune collects all of these stories in one place, eight tales that range from the earliest adventure in the Dune universe, to a story at the very end of Frank Herbert's grand future history. The stories are standalone, and should be enjoyable as they are, but the chronology at the end of this book shows exactly how they fit into the overall epic.

The Butlerian Jihad Period

Hunting Harkonnens

Introduction

By the time we turned in the Legends of Dune trilogy, which chronicles the epic Butlerian Jihad, we were introducing Dune fans to history ten thousand years prior to the events in the novel *Dune*. We felt this deserved an appetizer that would ease readers into an epoch that would span more than two centuries, establishing the origins of much of the Dune universe.

"Hunting Harkonnens" is our short-story introduction to the world of the Butlerian Jihad. During one of our book-signing tours, we found ourselves stuck for several hours in the Los Angeles train station. There, while sitting on an uncomfortable wooden bench larger than a church pew, we brainstormed all of "Hunting Harkonnens." In this preliminary tale, which lays the foundations of the holy war between humans and thinking machines, we introduced readers to the ancestors of the Atreides and the Harkonnens, and to the evil machines with human minds that Frank Herbert mentioned in *Dune*.

Passing a laptop computer back and forth, the two of us blocked out the story in detail, scene by scene. Then, like team managers picking baseball players during a draft, we each chose the scenes that interested us. Shortly after returning home from the tour, we wrote our parts of the story, swapped computer disks (yes, that's how long ago it was), and rewrote each other's work, sending the changes to each other by mail until we were satisfied with the end result.

Hunting Harkonnens

I

The Harkonnen space yacht left the family-held industries on Hagal and crossed the interstellar gulf toward Salusa Secundus. The streamlined vessel flew silently, in contrast to the fusillade of angry shouts inside the cockpit.

Stern, hard-line Ulf Harkonnen piloted the yacht, concentrating on the hazards of space and the constant threat of thinking machines, though he kept lecturing his twenty-one-year-old son, Piers. Ulf's wife Katarina, too gentle a soul to be worthy of the Harkonnen name, asserted that the quarrel had gone on long enough. "Further criticism and shouting will serve no purpose, Ulf."

Vehemently, the elder Harkonnen disagreed.

Piers sat fuming, unrepentant; he was not cut out for the cutthroat practices his noble family expected, no matter how much his father tried to bully them into him. He knew Ulf would browbeat and humiliate him all the way home. The gruff older man refused to consider that his son's ideas for more humane methods might actually be more efficient than the inflexible, domineering ways.

Clutching the ship controls as if in a death grip, Ulf growled at his son, "*Thinking machines* are efficient. Humans, especially riff-raff like our slaves on Hagal, are meant to be used. I doubt you'll ever get that through your skull." He shook his large, squarish head. "Sometimes, Piers, I think I should clean up the gene pool by eliminating you."

"Then why don't you?" Piers snapped, defiant. His father believed in forceful decisions, every question with a black-and-white answer, and that belittling his son would drive him to do better.

"I can't, because your brother Xavier is too young to be the Harkonnen heir, so you're the only choice I have … for the time being. I keep hoping you'll understand your responsibility to our family. You're a noble, meant to command, not to show the workers how soft you can be."

Katarina pleaded, "Ulf, you may not agree with the changes Piers made on Hagal, but at least he thought it through and was trying a new process. Given time it might have led to improved productivity."

"And meanwhile the Harkonnen family goes bankrupt?" Ulf held a thick finger toward his son as if it were a weapon. "Piers, those people took terrible advantage of you, and you're lucky I arrived in time to stop the damage. When I provide you with detailed instructions on how our family holdings are to be run, I do not expect you to come up with a 'better' idea."

"Is your mind so fossilized that you can't accept new ideas?" Piers asked.

"Your instincts are faulty, and you have a very naïve view of human nature." Ulf shook his head, growling in disappointment. "He takes after you, Katarina—that's his main problem." Like his mother, Piers had a narrow face, full lips and a delicate expression … quite different from Ulf's shaggy gray hair framing a blunt-featured face. "You would have been a better poet than a Harkonnen."

That was meant to be a grave insult, but Piers secretly agreed. The young man had always enjoyed reading histories of the Old Empire, days of decadence and ennui before the thinking machines had conquered many civilized solar systems. Piers would have fit into those times well as a writer, a storyteller.

"I gave you an opportunity, son, hoping that I could depend on you. But I have had my answer." The elder Harkonnen stood clenching his large, callused fists. "This whole trip has been a waste."

8

Katarina caressed her husband's broad back, trying to calm him. "Ulf, we're passing near the Caladan system. You talked about stopping there to investigate the possibility of new holdings … maybe fishing operations?"

Ulf hunched his shoulders. "All right, we'll divert to Caladan and take a look." He snapped his head up. "But in the meantime, I want this disgrace of a son sealed in the lifepod chamber. It's the closest thing to a brig onboard. He needs to learn his lesson, take his responsibilities seriously, or he will never be a true Harkonnen."

II

As he sulked inside his improvised cell, with its cream-colored walls and silver instrument panels, Piers stared out the small porthole window. He hated arguments with his stubborn father. The rigid old ways of the Harkonnen family were not always best. Instead of imposing tough conditions and harsh punishments, why not try treating workers with respect?

Workers. He remembered how his father had reacted to the word. "Next you'll want to call them employees. They are *slaves!*" Ulf had thundered as they stood in the overseer's office back on Hagal. "They have no rights."

"But they deserve rights," Piers responded. "They're human beings, not machines."

Ulf had barely contained his violence. "Perhaps I should beat you the way my father beat me, pounding contrition and responsibility into you. This isn't a game. You're leaving now, boy. Get on the ship."

Like a scolded child, Piers had done as he was commanded ....

He wished he could stand toe to toe with his father, just once. Every time he tried, though, Ulf made him feel that he had let the family down, as if he were a shirker who would waste their hard-won fortunes.

His father had entrusted him to manage the family holdings on Hagal, grooming him as the next head of the Harkonnen businesses. This assignment had been an important step for Piers, with complete authority over the sheet-diamond operations. A chance, a test. The implicit understanding was that he would operate the mines as they had always been run.

Harkonnens held the mining rights to all sheet diamonds on sparsely populated Hagal. The largest mine filled an entire canyon. Piers recalled how sunlight played off the glassy cliffs, dancing on the prismatic surfaces. He had never seen anything so beautiful.

The cliff faces were diamond sheets with blue-green quartz marking the perimeters, like irregular picture frames. Human-operated mining machines crawled along the cliffs like fat, silver insects: no artificial intelligence, and therefore considered safe. History had shown that even the most innocuous types of AI could ultimately turn against humans. Entire star systems were now under the control of diabolically smart machines, and in those dark sectors of the universe, human slaves followed the commands of mechanized masters.

At optimal spots on the shimmering cliffs, the mining machines would lock onto the surface with suction devices and separate the diamond material with sound waves at natural points of fissure; holding diamond sheets in their grasp, the dumb machines would make their way back down the cliff to loading areas.

It was an efficient process, but sometimes the sonic cutting procedure shattered the diamond sheets. Once Piers gave the slaves a stake in the profits, though, such mishaps occurred much less frequently, as if they took greater care after they received a vested interest.

Overseeing the Hagal operation, Piers had come up with the idea of letting the captive gangs work without typical Harkonnen regulations and close oversight. While some slaves accepted the incentive program, a number of problems did surface. With reduced supervision, some slaves ran away; others were disorganized or lazy, just waiting for someone to tell them what to do. Initially, productivity dropped, but he was sure the output would eventually meet and even exceed previous levels.

Before that could happen, though, his father had made an unannounced visit to Hagal. And Ulf Harkonnen wasn't interested in creative ideas or humanitarian improvements if profits were down ….

His parents had been forced to leave their younger son Xavier on Salusa with a pleasant old-school couple. "I shudder to think how the boy will turn out if *they* raise him. Emil and Lucille Tantor don't know how to be strict."

Eavesdropping, Piers knew why his manipulative father had left his little brother with the Tantors. Since the aging couple was

11

childless, wily Ulf was working his way into their good graces. He hoped the Tantors might eventually leave their estate to their dear "godson" Xavier.

Piers hated the way his father used people, whether they were slaves, other nobles, or members of his own family. It was disgusting. But now, trapped inside the cramped lifepod chamber, he could do nothing about it.

III

Programming made the thinking machines relentless and determined, but only the cruelty of a human mind could generate enough ruthless hatred to feed a war of extermination for a thousand years.

Though they were kept in reluctant thrall by the pervasive computer mind Omnius, the cymeks—hybrid machines with human minds—often bided their time by hunting between the stars. They could capture feral humans, bring them back to slavery on the Synchronized Worlds, or just kill them for sport ....

The leader of the cymeks, a general who had taken the imposing name of Agamemnon, had once led a group of tyrants to conquer the decaying Old Empire. As implacable soldiers in the cause, the tyrants had reprogrammed the subservient robots and computers to give them a thirst for conquest. When his mortal human body grew old and weak, Agamemnon had undergone a surgical process that removed his brain and implanted it within a preservation canister that he could install into varying mechanical bodies.

Agamemnon and his fellow tyrants had intended to rule for centuries ... but then the artificially aggressive computers stepped into power when they saw the chance, exploiting the tyrants' lack of diligence. The Omnius network then ruled the remnants of the Old Empire, subjugating the cymek tyrants along with the rest of already-downtrodden humanity.

For centuries, Agamemnon and his fellow conquerors had been forced to serve the computer evermind, with no chance of regaining their own rule. Their greatest source of amusement was in tracking down stray humans who had managed to maintain their independence from machine domination. Still, the cymek general found it a most unsatisfactory venting of his frustrations.

His brain canister had been installed inside a fast scout vessel that patrolled areas known to be inhabited by League humans. Six cymeks accompanied the general as their ships skirted the edge of a small solar system. They found little of interest, only one human-compatible world composed of mostly water.

Then Agamemnon's long-range sensors spotted another vessel. A *human* vessel.

He increased resolution and pointed out the target to his companions. Triangulating with their combined detection abilities, Agamemnon discerned that the lone ship was a small space yacht, its sophisticated configuration and style implying that its passengers were important members of the League, rich merchants ... perhaps even smug nobles, the most gratifying victims of all.

"Just what we've been waiting for," said Agamemnon.

The cymek ships adjusted course and accelerated. Connected through thoughtrodes, Agamemnon's brain flew his ship-body as if it were a large bird of prey, zeroing in on his helpless target. He also had a terrestrial walker stored aboard, a warrior form that could be used for planetary combat.

The first cymek shots took the League vessel completely by surprise. The doomed human pilot barely had time to take evasive maneuvers. Kinetic projectiles scraped the hull, pounding one of the engines, but the ship's defensive armor protected it against severe damage. Cymek ships swept past, strafing again with explosive projectiles, and the human yacht reeled, intact but disoriented.

"Careful, boys," Agamemnon said. "We don't want to destroy the prize."

Out on the outskirts of League space, far from the Synchronized Worlds, the feral humans obviously hadn't expected to encounter enemy predators, and the captain of this vessel had been particularly inattentive. Defeating him would be almost embarrassing. His cymek hunters would hope for a better challenge, a more entertaining pursuit ....

The human pilot got his damaged engine back online and increased speed down into the isolated system, fleeing toward the water world. In his wake, the human launched a flurry of intensely bright explosive shells that caused little physical damage, but sent pulses of confusing static through the machine sensors of the cymek ships. Agamemnon's cymek followers transmitted a series of imaginative curses. Surprisingly, the human victim responded in a gruff, defiant voice with equal venom and vigor.

Agamemnon chuckled to himself and sent a thought-command. This would be more fun. His attack ship burst forward like a wild and energetic horse, part of his imaginary body. "Give chase!" The cymeks, enjoying the game, swooped after the hapless human vessel.

The doomed pilot flew standard maneuvers to evade the pursuers. Agamemnon held back, trying to determine if the human was truly so inexperienced or just lulling the cymeks into an unwarranted sense of ease.

They plummeted toward the peaceful blue world—*Caladan*, according to the onboard database. The world reminded him of the blue irises his human eyes once had …. It had been so many centuries, the cymek general could recall few details of his original physical appearance.

Agamemnon could have transmitted an ultimatum to the pilot, but humans and cymeks knew the stakes in their long simmering war. The space yacht opened fire, a few pathetically weak blasts designed for shoving troublesome meteoroids out of the way rather than defending against overt military action. If this was a noble ship, it should have had much more serious offensive and defensive weapons. The cymeks laughed and closed in, perceiving no threat.

As soon as they approached, though, the desperate human pilot launched another flurry of explosives, apparently the same as the gnat-bite bombs he had launched previously, but Agamemnon detected slight fluctuations. "Caution, I suspect—"

Four proximity mines, each a space charge ten times as powerful as the first artillery, detonated with huge shock waves. Two of the cymek hunters suffered external damage; one was completely destroyed.

Agamemnon lost his patience. "Back off! Engage ship defenses!"

But the yacht pilot fired no more explosives. With one of the surviving cymeks moving only sluggishly, the human could easily have taken him out. Since he did not, the human prey must have no further weapons available. Or was it another trick?

"Don't underestimate the vermin."

Agamemnon had hoped to take the feral humans captive, delivering them to Omnius for experiments or analysis, since "wild" specimens were considered different from those raised for generations in captivity. But, angry at the pointless loss of one of his over-eager companions, the general decided it was just too much trouble.

"Vaporize that ship," he transmitted to his five remaining followers. Without waiting for the other cymeks to join him, Agamemnon opened fire.

IV

Inside the lifepod, Piers could only watch in horror and wait to die. The enemy cymeks pounded them again. In the cockpit, his father shouted curses, and his mother did her best at the weapons station. Their eyes betrayed no fear, only showed strong determination. Harkonnens did not die easily.

Ulf had insisted on installing the best armor and defensive systems available, always suspicious, always ready to fight against any threat. But this lone yacht could not withstand the concerted attack from seven fully armed and aggressive cymek marauders.

Sealed inside the dim compartment, Piers could do nothing to help. He watched the attacking machines through a porthole, sure they could not hold out long. Even his father, who refused to bow to defeat, looked as if he had no tricks remaining to him.

Sensing the imminent kill, the cymeks streaked closer. Piers heard repeated thumps reverberating in the vessel. Through the hatch porthole, Piers saw his mother and father gesturing desperately at one another.

Another cymek blast finally breached the protective plates and damaged the yacht's engines as the vessel careened toward the not-close-enough planet with broad blue seas and white lacings of clouds. Sparks flew on the bridge, and the wounded ship began to tumble.

Ulf Harkonnen shouted something at his wife, then lurched toward the lifepod, trying to keep his balance. Katarina called after him. Piers couldn't figure out what they were arguing about; the ship was doomed.

Cymek weapons fire rocked the vessel with a dull concussion, sending Ulf skidding across the deck. Even the augmented hull armor could not withstand much more. The elder Harkonnen struggled to his feet at the lifepod hatch, and Piers suddenly realized that he wanted to unlock the chamber and get both of them inside with their son.

Piers read his mother's lips as she shouted, "No time!"

The lifepod's instrument panel flashed and began running through test cycles. Piers hammered on the hatch, but they had sealed him inside. He couldn't get out to help them.

While Ulf tried frantically to work the hatch controls, Katarina raced for the panel on the wall and slapped the activation switch. While Ulf turned to his wife in astonishment and dismay, Katarina mouthed a desperate farewell to her son.

With a lurch, the lifepod shot into space, away from the doomed space yacht.

Acceleration threw Piers to the deck, but he scrambled to his knees, to the observation port. Behind him, as the lifepod tumbled recklessly through space, the cymek marauders opened fire again and again, six angry thinking machines combining their destructive power.

The Harkonnen ship erupted in a sequence of explosions into a dazzling fireball, which dissipated into the cluttered vacuum … snuffed out along with the lives of his parents.

Like a cannonball, the lifepod tore into the atmosphere of Caladan, spraying red sparks of reentry as it zoomed toward the blue oceans on the sunlit side of the planet.

Piers struggled with the crude emergency controls in an effort to maneuver, but the small ship didn't respond, as if it were a machine rebelling against its human master. At this rate of speed, he couldn't possibly survive.

The young Harkonnen heir took an agonized breath and tapped pressure pads to alter the thruster pattern. He had little experience in piloting, though his father had insisted that he learn; previously, the skill had not been a priority for Piers, but now he had to figure out the systems without delay.

Looking back, he saw he was being pursued by one of the cymek fighter ships. The spray of reentry sparks increased, like iron filings from a grinding stone. The pursuer's exploding projectiles rocked the atmosphere around him without making direct hits.

Piers sped low over an isolated landmass toward a snowy mountain ridge, with the vicious cymek on his tail, still shooting. Sparkling glaciers girdled the jagged peaks. One of the enemy's kinetic projectiles hit a high ridge, shattering ice and rock. Piers closed his eyes and boldly—without a choice—flew through the debris, heard it pummeling the lifepod. And he barely survived.

Just after he scraped over the ridge, he heard a tremendous explosion and saw the sky behind him light up in a flash of bright orange. The mechanical pursuer had gone out of control. Destroyed, just like his parents and their spacecraft ....

But Piers knew there were other enemies, and probably not far away.

V

Agamemnon and his cymeks clustered around the space yacht's wreckage in unstable orbit, while mapping the trajectory of the single ejected lifepod. They marked where it crossed the atmosphere, how fast it descended, and where it would probably land. The general was in no hurry—after all, where could the lone survivor go on this primitive world?

Without orders, though, the one cymek damaged by proximity mines shot after the lifepod, hungry for revenge. "General Agamemnon, I intend to make this kill on my own." Angrily, the cymek leader paused, then agreed. "Go, you get the first shot. But the rest of us won't wait for long." The cymek leader held the rest of them back until he could finish his analysis.

Agamemnon played the distress signal the noble pilot had transmitted shortly before his destruction. The words were encoded, but not with a very sophisticated cipher; the cymek's onboard AI systems translated it easily. "This is Lord Ulf Harkonnen, en route from our holdings at Hagal. We are under attack by thinking machines. There is not much chance we will survive."

Such amazing powers of prediction. Agamemnon assumed the survivor aboard the lifepod must also be a member of the noble family, if not the lord himself.

A thousand years ago, when Agamemnon and his nineteen co-conspirators had overthrown the Old Empire, a group of outlying planets had banded together to form the League of Nobles. They had defended themselves against the tyrants, maintaining their defense against Omnius and his thinking machines. Computers did not hold grudges or gain vengeance ... but the cymeks had human minds and human emotions.

If the survivor in the lifepod down on Caladan was a member of the defiant League of Nobles, the cymek general wanted to participate personally in his interrogation, torture, and ultimate execution.

Within minutes, however, he received a last-second transmission just before the cymek pursuer crashed on the surface.

"A foolish mission. Next time I want it done right," Agamemnon said. "Go, find him before he can hide in the wilderness. I give the hunt to the four of you—and a challenge. A reward to the cymek who finds and kills the prey first."

The other cymek ships streaked away from the debris field, heading like hot bullets into the cloudy skies. The human escapee, unarmed in his barely maneuverable lifepod, certainly would not last long.

VI

Abruptly the lifepod shuddered, and a warning siren sounded. Digital and crystal instruments sparked on the panel. Piers tried to interpret them, adjusting the clumsy controls of the careening vessel, then looked up through the porthole to see brown-and-white slopes ahead, bleak frozen hillsides with patches of snow, dark forests. In the last instant, he pulled up, just enough—

The lifepod scraped tall, dark-needled trees and crashed into high tundra covered by only a thin blanket of snow. The impact bounced the pod back into the air, spinning it around for a second plunge into the patchy forest.

In his energy harness, Piers rolled and shouted, trying to survive but expecting the worst. Cushioning bubblefoam squirted all around him just before the first impact, padding his body from the worst injuries. Then the pod crashed again, ripping up snow and frozen dirt. The pod finally came to rest, groaning and hissing.

The bubblefoam dissolved as Piers picked himself up and wiped the fizzing slime from his clothes and hands and hair. He was too shaken to feel pain and couldn't take the time to evaluate his injuries.

He knew his parents were dead, their ship destroyed. He hoped his blurred vision was from blood in his eyes, not tears. He was a Harkonnen, after all. His father would have struck him across the cheek for showing cowardly emotion. Ulf had managed to damage the enemy in a fruitless attack, but there were still more cymeks up there. No doubt they would come hunting for him.

Piers fought down panic, turned it into a hard, instant assessment of his situation. If he had any hope of surviving, circumstances forced him to respond with decisiveness, even ruthlessness—the Harkonnen way. And he wouldn't have much time.

The lifepod contained a few survival supplies, but he couldn't stay here. The cymeks would zero in on the vessel and come to finish the job. Once he ran, he would have no chance to return.

Piers grabbed a medical kit and all the ration packs he could carry, stuffing them into a flexible sack. He popped the lifepod's hatch and crawled out, smelling the smoke and hearing the crackle of a few gasping fires ignited by the heat of impact. He took a deep breath of cold, biting air then, closing the hatch behind him, he staggered away from the smoking pod, crunching through slushy snow into the meager shelter of dark conifers. He wanted to get as far away as possible before pausing to consider his next step.

In a situation like this, his father would have been concerned about the family holdings, the Hagal mines. With Piers and his parents gone, who would run the business and keep the Harkonnen family strong? Right now, though, the young man was more worried for his own survival. He had never fit in with family business philosophies anyway.

Hearing a high-pitched roar, he gazed into the sky and saw four flaming white trails coming toward him like targeted munitions. Cymek landers. Hunters. The machines with human minds would track him down in the desolate wilderness.

As the danger suddenly came closer to home, Piers saw he was leaving deep tracks in the snow. Blood dripped from a nasty cut on his left wrist; more scarlet splashed from another injury on his forehead. He might as well be leaving a road map for the enemy to follow.

His father had said it in a stern, impatient voice, but the lesson was valuable nevertheless: *Be aware of all facets of a situation. Just because something is quiet does not mean it isn't dangerous. Do not trust your safety at any moment.*

Under the trees, listening to the roar as cymeks converged over his pod's crash-down coordinates, Piers slathered wound sealant on his injuries to stop the bleeding. *A moment's hurry can cause far more damage than a moment's delay to plan ahead.*

He abruptly changed direction, selecting a clear area where trees had sheltered the ground from the snow and rocks. He moved over the rocky surface in a deliberately chaotic course, hoping to throw off pursuit. He had no weapons, no knowledge of the terrain … and no intention of giving up.

Piers climbed higher up the sloping ground, and the snow grew thicker where the trees became sparse. When he reached a clearing, he caught his breath and looked back to see that cymek landers had converged at his lifepod. Still not far enough away, but still without any place to run.

Watching in horrified fascination, Piers saw mobile, resilient walker-forms emerge from the landed ships: adaptable mechanical bodies to carry cymek brain canisters across a variety of environments. Like angry crabs, the cymeks crawled over the sealed wreckage, using cutter claws and white-hot flamers to tear open the hull. When they found no one inside, they literally ripped the lifepod apart.

The walker-forms stalked around the pod, their optic threads gleaming with a variety of sensors. They scanned his footprints in the snow, moved to where their prey had paused to apply his medical pack. The cymek scanners could easily pick up his footprints in the dirt, thermal traces from his body heat, any number of clues. Unerringly, they set out across the bare ground toward where he had chosen to flee.

Chiding himself for the momentary panic that had made him leave such an obvious trail, Piers broke into a full run uphill, always looking for a place to hide, a weapon to use. He tried to ignore his hammering heart and his difficulty breathing in this cold, rugged environment of Caladan. He crashed into another thicket of the dark pines, always climbing. The slope became steeper, but because of the dense conifers, he couldn't see exactly where he was going or how close he might be to the top of a ridge.

He saw sticks, rocks, but nothing that would be an effective weapon against the mechanical monsters, no way to defend himself against the horrific machines. But Piers was, after all, a Harkonnen, and he would not give up. He would hurt them if he could. At the very least, he would offer them a fine chase.

Far to his rear, Piers heard crashing sounds, cracking trees, and imagined the cymeks clearing a path for their armored bodies. Judging from the smoke, they must be setting the forest on fire as well. Good—that way they would ruin the subtleties of his trail.

He kept running as the ground became rockier, with patches of ice spreading out on steep slopes. Precariously balanced snow clung to the mountain, ready to break loose at any moment. The trees at this elevation were bent and twisted, and he smelled a foul sulfurous taint in the air. At his feet he saw tiny bubbling puddles, suffused with yellow.

He furrowed his brows, pondering what this could mean. A thermal area. He had read about such places in his studies, esoteric geological anomalies that his father had forced him to learn before sending him to the mining operations on Hagal. This would be a region of volcanic activity with hot springs, geysers, fumaroles … a dangerous place, but one that offered opportunities against large opponents.

Piers ran toward the strong smell and the thickening mist, hoping this would give him an advantage. Cymeks did not use eyes like humans did, and their sensors were delicate, sensitive to different parts of the spectrum. In some cases, it gave the machine pursuers an incredible advantage. Here, though, with the wild plumes of heat and the rocky, sterile ground, the cymeks could not use their scanners to pick up residual traces from his footprints.

He raced through the misty, humid no-man's-land of rocks, snow patches, crusty bare earth, trying to throw off pursuit and seeking a place to hide, or defend. After hours of headlong flight, he collapsed on a warm boulder encrusted with orange lichen next to a hissing steam vent. More than anything else, he wanted to curl up under a rocky overhang next to one of the hot springs, remaining hidden long enough to sleep for a few hours.

But cymeks did not require sleep. All of their life-support needs were taken care of with restorative electrafluid that kept them alive in their preservation canisters. They would keep pursuing him without pause.

Piers cracked open the food rations and gobbled two high-energy wafers, but he forced himself to set off again before he felt any resurgence of stamina. He had to press his advantage, not lose any ground.

Using his hands and feet now, Piers climbed steeper rocks. His fingers became powdery with yellow sulfur. He chose the steepest terrain, hoping it would prove difficult for the cymek walker bodies, but it also slowed him down.

The wind began to pick up, and Piers felt it against his face, alternate blasts of warm and cold. The mists cleared in patches, and suddenly the landscape was revealed around him. He looked back toward the last remnants of conifer forests, jutting rocks, and the bubbling mineral pools far beneath him.

Then he saw one of the cymek walker-forms, alone, stalking him. The other three must have separated, circling in their hunt, as if it were some sort of game. The mechanical body glistened silver in the sudden wash of afternoon light. Searching.

Piers knew he was exposed and unprotected on the rocky slope; he slammed his body tight against the rocks, hoping to remain unseen. But within seconds, the cymek had targeted its prey. The mechanical walker unleashed a fiery projectile, a splattering globule of flaming gel that missed Piers and struck the rock, clinging fire.

He scrambled up the rock, finding a new surge of energy. Scuttling rapidly, the cymek negotiated the rough slope, no longer wasting time on the tedious job of tracking the human.

Piers was trapped, with precipitous drop-offs and hot sulfurous pools on the left and right and a steep, smooth snowfield crusted with yellow contaminants above him. Once he got to the top of the ridge, perhaps he could throw rocks, somehow dislodge the cymek below him. He saw no other option.

Clawing with his hands and struggling for footholds, Piers worked his way up the slick glacier field. His shoes punched through the crust, sinking into cold snow up to his knees. His fingers soon grew numb and red. The frigid air seared his lungs, but he scrambled faster, farther. His domineering father would have sneered at him for worrying about mere physical discomfort in a time of such urgency. The glacier seemed to go on forever, though he could see the top, a sheer razor edge on the crest.

The machine hunters must have split up, and perhaps he had eluded the other three among the thermal plumes and crumbling rocks. Unable to find his tracks, they would be combing the ground ... relentless, as machines always were. Only one of the cymeks had found him, apparently by accident.

Even so, a single monstrous enemy was more than enough to kill him, and this one would be in radio contact with the others. Already they must be coming this way. But this one seemed eager to kill Piers all by itself.

Below, the cymek reached the base of the ice field, scanned for a moment, and then scuttled up. Its long legs stabbed into the snow, climbing faster than any human could hope to run.

The cymek paused, rocked back, then launched another gel-fire projectile. Piers burrowed into the snow, and the hot explosive ripped a crater barely an arm's length away from him. The violent impact caused the steep and precarious snowfield to tremble and shift. Around him, the crust began to break apart like a peeling scab. Taking a chance, he kicked hard at one of the hard slabs of packed snow, hoping to send it tumbling down to strike his enemy, but the frozen surface jammed tight again, squeaking and groaning, then falling silent. With a deep breath, he climbed upward again.

As the cymek closed the gap, Piers noticed a rocky outcropping that protruded from the snow. He would scramble up there and make his stand. Maybe he could throw boulders at the machine, though he had no illusions about how effective that would be.

Only a fool leaves himself without options, Ulf Harkonnen would have said.

Piers grumbled at the memory. "At least I survived longer than you did, Father."

Then, to his astonishment, at the crest of the glacier he saw a group of figures that looked … *human!* He counted dozens of people who stood at the top of the snowfield. They shouted incomprehensible curses at the cymek.

The silhouetted strangers lifted large cylinders—weapons of some sort?—and began to beat on them. Loud booming sounds echoed across the mountains like thunderclaps, explosions. *Drums.*

The strangers pounded on their noisemakers. They had no apparent rhythm at first, but then the pulses combined into a resonance, an echoing boom that set the whole snowfield trembling.

Cracks widened atop the ice, and the glacier began to shift. The massive cymek walker struggled for purchase as the frozen ground began to slide.

Seeing what was about to happen, Piers dove for the rock outcropping, sheltering himself in a pocket walled off by thick stone on each side. He held on just as the snow broke free with a hissing, tumbling roar.

The avalanche struck the cymek like a white tidal wave, bowling over the walker-form, knocking and battering it against other rocks. As the enemy machine crashed down the slope, Piers closed his eyes and waited for the rumbling roar to reach its crescendo and then taper off.

When he finally emerged, amazed to be alive, the air itself sparkled with ice crystals thrown into the sky. While the snowpack undoubtedly remained unstable, the strange people charged pell-mell down the broken snow and ice, yelling excitedly like hunters who had just bagged an impressive quarry.

Still unable to believe what he was seeing, Piers stood atop the boulders. And then he spotted the twitching and battered cymek far down the slope, toppled onto its back. The avalanche had struck it with a destructive force equivalent to a heavy weapon. The cymek had been bashed, dented, and twisted, but still its mechanical limbs attempted to haul the walker-form upright.

Although the primitive humans wore drab survival garb made of scavenged materials, they carried sophisticated tools, more than just spears or clubs. Four young natives hurried to the edge of the broken icefield and the trees—scouts?—and they kept watch, wary of other cymeks.

The remaining humans fell like hyenas upon the crippled cymek, wielding cutters and grappling wrenches. Was the mechanical hunter calling for help from its three comrades? The natives quickly bashed the transmitter antennas on the walker body then, with startling efficiency they dismantled the walker's struggling legs. The cymek weapon arm flickered in an attempt to launch another flaming projectile, but the Caladan primitives quickly disconnected the components.

From the cymek's speakerpatch came a volley of angry threats and curses, but the humans paid no attention, showing no fear. They worked diligently to disconnect the hydraulics, fiber cables, neurelectronics, setting each piece aside like valuable scrap material. They

28

left the cymek's brain canister exposed, the traitorous human mind disembodied once again, though this time not by its own volition.

Numb, Piers looked at the oddly harmless-looking canister that held the cymek's mind. The natives did not destroy it immediately, but seemed to have other plans. They held it up like a trophy.

Full of questions, Piers made his way down the shifting surface of broken snow. The natives looked up at him as he approached, showing curiosity without threat. They spoke a gibberish language that he could not comprehend.

"Who are you?" Piers asked in standard Galach, hoping that someone here would understand him.

One of the men, a gaunt old fellow with a short reddish beard and lighter skin than his companions, gestured toward Piers in happy victory. He stood in front of Piers, pounded himself on the chest. "Tiddoc."

"Piers Harkonnen." He responded, then decided to simplify, "Piers."

"Good, Piers. Thank you," he said in recognizable Galach, but with a thick accent. Seeing the young man's surprise, Tiddoc spoke slowly, as if fishing the right words out of his memory. "Our tongue has Galach roots from the Zensunni Wanderers, who fled the League long ago. For years I worked in cities of the noblemen, performing menial tasks. I picked up words here and there."

Paralyzed and immobile, the captured enemy cymek continued to snarl insults through an integrated speakerpatch as the Caladan natives used two of the amputated walker legs as support rods, lashing the brain canister so that it dangled between the poles like some captured wild beast. Two of the strongest-looking natives put the metal rods over their shoulders and began to march back up the slope. The other natives gathered up the components they could carry and climbed the rough mountainside.

"Come with us," Tiddoc said.

Piers had no option but to follow them.

VII

As Piers followed the rugged men uphill, one of his knees throbbed with each step, and his back stiffened until it burned. He had not yet had time to accept the deaths of his parents. He missed his mother, for her kind attentions, her intelligence. Katarina had saved his life, launching the lifepod before the cymeks could destroy the space yacht.

In a way, Piers even missed his father. Despite Ulf's gruffness, he had only wanted the best for his sons, harshly focused on his responsibilities for Harkonnen holdings. Advancing the family fortunes was always paramount. Now it seemed that his little brother Xavier was all that remained of the Harkonnen bloodline. Piers had little hope that he would ever get away from Caladan ... but at least he had survived this long.

He limped up the steep slope, trying to keep pace with the agile natives. Inside its preservation canister, the evil cymek brain sloshed as the primitives carried it. Staticky shouts came from the canister's speakerpatch, first in standard Galach, then in other languages. Tiddoc and the natives seemed to find it amusing.

The natives paid little attention to the disembodied brain, except to glare at it and bare their teeth. The red-bearded old man was the most demonstrative. In addition to menacing facial expressions, he made threatening gestures with a cutting tool, swinging it close to the canister's sensors, which only served to agitate the captive brain more. Obviously they had encountered cymeks before and knew how to fight them.

But he was concerned about the other three mechanical hunters. They would not give up the pursuit—and once they found the avalanche site and the dismantled walker-form, the cymeks could track the natives here. Unless the captured one had not been able to signal for help before the avalanche had swept it away. Cymeks did not like to admit weakness.

Piers looked around for any fortifications the people had made. Ahead, overhanging ice formed a giant roof that sheltered a settlement. The primitives had made their camp in a large area melted out by thermal vents in the ground. Women and children bustled among rock huts, performing chores, pausing to look at the approaching party. The people wore thick clothing, boots, and hats lined with fur from unknown local animals. Piers heard the yelping of animals, saw furry white creatures near the dwellings.

Beyond the shelter of the overhang, steam roiled up through thick layers of ice and snow, accompanied by heat bubbles from mudpots and geysers. As Piers followed the tribe down narrow rock steps toward the settlement, he marveled at the stunning contrast of fire and ice. Occasional droplets rained down from the ceiling of the dome, slowly melting, but when Piers looked up at the blue ice overhead, he thought the glacier—and the settlement—had been here for a long time ....

When abrupt darkness fell like a curtain drawn in front of the sun, the native Caladan women used jagged pieces of wood to build a large fire on a rocky area at the center of the settlement. Scouts went out on patrol to keep watch for other cymek hunters while the rest of the tribe settled down to celebrate. The men brought hunks of fresh meat from other hunts and speared them on long metal spits over the fire.

They placed the captive cymek's brain canister off to one side, in the ice, and ignored it.

Speaking to one another in their guttural tongue, the natives sat on furs around the fire and passed the food around, sharing with their visitor. Piers found the meat too gamey for his liking, but he finished a large hunk, not wanting to insult his hosts. He was famished, and supplemented his meal with part of a ration bar he had salvaged from the lifepod; he offered the rest of the packaged food to his rescuers, and they eagerly accepted.

Following the meal, Tiddoc and his people sat around the story fire, telling ancient parables and adventures in their native tongue.

During the sharing, the tribesmen passed around gourds of a potent beverage. Wrapped in a fur to ward off the chill air, Piers drank, and felt warm in his belly. At intervals, the old man translated for Piers, relating tales of the downtrodden Zensunni who had fled the machine takeovers, as well as slavery in the League of Nobles.

A little tipsy, Piers defended the League and their continuing fight against the thinking machines, though he sympathized with the unpleasant plight of the Buddislamic slaves on Poritrin, Zanbar, and other League Worlds. While Tiddoc struggled to translate, Piers told of epic battles against the evil Omnius and his aggressive robots and cymeks.

And, with a thick voice, he told how his own ship had been destroyed, his parents killed ....

Tiddoc gestured to the cymek brain canister. "Come. The feasting is done. Now we finish our machine war. The people have been looking forward to this." He shouted something in his own language, and two men lifted the canister by its improvised poles. The cymek grumbled from its speakerpatch, but it had run out of effective curses.

Several women lit torches from the central fire and led the way up a path from the dripping glacier overhang. Full of good cheer, the natives marched away, carrying the impotent enemy brain. The cymek hurled threats in every language it could think of, but the primitives only laughed at it.

"What are you doing?" the cymek demanded. Controlling his last functional thoughtrodes, the disembodied brain twisted in its container. "Stop! We will crush you all!"

Piers followed them over a ridge and down a slope to where the air reeked of sulfur and the porous rock grew warm underfoot. Carrying the helpless cymek, the group paused at a steaming hole in the rock and stood chattering and laughing. They held the brain canister over the ominous opening.

Piers bent closer to the hole, curious, but Tiddoc yanked him away. The red-bearded elder wore an eerie smile in the torchlight.

A rumble sounded deep below, and with a preliminary spurt of hot spray, a geyser erupted, a scalding jet that parboiled the cymek's brain. The enemy's curses turned to shrieks, followed by babbling sounds and disjointed pain that trickled out of the damaged speakerpatch.

When the geyser subsided, the delirious cymek cried and gibbered. Moments later the geyser erupted again, and the speake patch unleashed hideous howls that sent shudders down Piers's spine.

Even though this monster had tried to kill him, had taken part in the murder of his parents, Piers could not tolerate hearing its misery anymore. When the boiling jet subsided again, he took a rock and smashed the speaker, disconnecting it.

But the natives continued to hold the agonized brain over the geyser hole, and when the scalding spray gushed out a third time, the cymek screamed in silence, until it was boiled alive in its electrafluid.

The natives then cracked the canister open on a rock and devoured the hot, cooked contents.

VIII

The rock hut was warm and marginally comfortable, but Piers slept poorly, unable to put the horrific images out of his mind. When he finally dreamed, he saw himself strapped to poles while the natives held him over the geyser hole. He heard boiling water rushing toward him, and he awoke with a scream caught in his throat.

Outside, he heard only the howl of an animal, then silence. Then mechanical sounds.

He stumbled to the entrance of the hut and peered outside into the cold, sulfur-smelling air. Now the furry guard animals howled. The primitives shouted and stirred in their encampment. The scouts had been watching.

In a slit of grayish, misty sky between the ground and the icy overhang Piers saw four aircraft approaching with insect-machine noises, their engines glowing in the predawn sky. *Cymeks!*

Tiddoc and the natives fled their stone huts, grabbing torches, weapons. Piers ran out, anxious to help.

The cymek ships landed in the nearby rock field and opened hatches, each one disgorging an armed walker body. The crablike warrior machines marched downslope with alarming speed. Ahead, the primitives scattered, hooting, waving torches, taunting the enemy.

One of the cymeks launched a rocket of gelfire, which exploded and collapsed part of the arched, glacier ceiling. Shards of ice tumbled down, smashing the evacuated stone huts.

Tiddoc and the villagers scampered out of the way as if it were a game, gesturing for Piers to follow as they hurried along the path they had taken the night before, onto the geyser field. In daylight Piers saw that it was a broad, gently sloped area of boiling mudpots and hot springs. Fumaroles and geysers belched repeatedly, filling the air with foul steam and heat plumes. Shouting, cursing, the people split up, following instinctive routes across the crusty ground. The natives' supposed panic was a strangely organized action, like a cat and mouse game. Were they luring the enemy? They seemed to have a plan, a hunt of their own.

Piers ran along with them, ducking as the four cymek walkers shot projectiles into the hissing thermal area. Their mechanical bodies plodded forward like heavy spiders on the uncertain ground. For sophisticated machines, their aim was terrible. The cymeks' optic threads and thermal sensors must be nearly blinded in the chaos of heat signatures.

Tiddoc hurled a spear, which clanked on the head turret of the largest cymek walker. Agitated, the machine-creature bellowed through a speakerpatch, "You cannot escape Agamemnon!" The other three cymeks scrambled along behind it.

Piers shuddered. All free humans knew the famous general of Omnius's army, one of the brutal original tyrants.

With a lucky shot, one of the enemy machines blasted a young man who danced too close to the weapon arm, and his twitching, burning body writhed on the ground. The Caladan natives, looking angry and vengeful, tightened their ranks and worked harder against the cymeks.

Light-footed, the primitives raced across the volcanically active area. The cymeks, oblivious to the trap, charged after their prey, smashing salty encrustations, pursuing the natives into the reeking mists. They shot more blobs of gelfire, fired explosive projectiles.

Tiddoc and the natives kept hooting and shouting, defiant. Two of the smaller cymeks surged forward into a crater-pocked geyser field. The waving, taunting primitives stopped and turned, expectant.

The thin shell of hardened ground cracked, split. The two mechanical walker-forms tried to skitter backward, but the surface gave way beneath them, breaking apart. Both cymeks plunged through the dangerous ground and tumbled screaming into roiling sulfur cauldrons.

Piers joined Tiddoc and the other humans in their loud cheer.

Unexpectedly, a furious geyser blast rocketed out of the ground next to a third cymek attacker, scalding the brain canister. Its thoughtrodes damaged, the mechanical behemoth veered away and stumbled around in confusion. The cymek fell to its articulated knees, the electrafluid in its stained brain canister glowing blue as it focused its mental energy.

Tiddoc tossed a small, homemade explosive onto the ground, like a crude grenade. The detonation caused no further damage to the armored walker, but the ground crust fractured. While the wounded mechanical enemy reeled, disoriented, the surface gave way. The third cymek joined the others in the molten mud.

Agamemnon kept advancing toward the retreating humans, as if scorning his incompetent underlings. The lead cymek stalked unwavering toward old Tiddoc. The red-bearded man and his companions threw their spears and more crude explosives, but the mechanical general did not flinch. Behind them and on the sides lay superheated soil, while the immense cymek blocked their only avenue of escape.

On impulse, Piers ran in front of the lead cymek, shouting to distract it. He snatched up a discarded spear and thumped it against one of the tall walker legs. "Agamemnon! You murdered my parents!"

To his surprise, the cymek general swiveled its head turret, and thermal sensors locked onto the upstart human's form. "A feisty one!" the monster said with considerable amusement. "You are the vermin we have been chasing."

"I am a Harkonnen nobleman!" Piers shouted. He swung the spear like a cudgel at the brain canister. He struck the thick armor plaz with a blow hard enough to rattle his bones—but he left only a tiny nick on the protective canister.

The cymek bellowed a laugh. One of Agamemnon's clawed legs grabbed Piers, yanked away the spear. The young man felt the sharp claw tighten around his torso. He was dimly aware of Tiddoc howling—

Then suddenly the crust gave way beneath the heavy cymek walker. Frothing mud gushed upward, and Agamemnon tumbled into a boiling geyser pit, still clutching his human victim. Superheated steam blasted upward, eradicating all signs of Piers and the last machine invader.

IX

Alive and angry, Agamemnon reinstalled himself in an intact spaceship lander and departed from the watery world. With his heavily protected walker body, he had clamped onto the edges of the fuming pit, endured the steam blasts without falling into the molten mud. The people rallied, hurled more explosives at him, and Agamemnon despised himself for being forced to retreat. Already damaged, his walker-form limped back to the landed spacecraft. Systems onboard reconfigured his brain canister to the ship's controls; he discarded the ruined walker body, leaving it as scrap on the cursed surface of Caladan.

The only survivor of his cymek squad, Agamemnon left the unremarkable world behind. He would return to Earth, and the computer evermind Omnius, and make his report.

At this point, he was at liberty to create whatever explanation he chose. Omnius would never suspect him of lying: Such things simply did not occur to the all-pervasive computer. But the cymek general had a human brain ....

As Agamemnon flew out into open space, he would have a long time to think of appropriate explanations and shift the blame. He would include his version of the events in his ever-growing memoirs recorded in the machine database.

Fortunately, the all-powerful and all-seeing evermind simply wanted information and an accurate recounting of all events. Making excuses was a purely human weakness.

X

On the League capital world of Salusa Secundus, a young boy looked up at dark-skinned Emil Tantor, a wealthy and influential noblemen. They stood on the front lawn of the sprawling Tantor estate, with the tallest buildings of the city visible in the distance. It was early evening, with lights twinkling on in the palatial homes that dotted the hills.

Ulf Harkonnen's distress signal had finally been intercepted, and Emil Tantor had brought the boy the terrible news about his parents and brother. More casualties in the long-standing war against the thinking machines.

Young Xavier Harkonnen bowed his head, but refused to cry. The kindly nobleman touched his shoulder and spoke deep-throated, gentle words. "Will you have me, and Lucille, as your foster parents? I think it is what your father wanted, when he left you in our care."

Xavier looked into his brown eyes, nodded.

"You'll grow into a fine young man," Tantor said, "one to make your brother and parents proud. We will do our best to raise you right, to teach you honor and responsibility. You will make the Harkonnen name shine in the annals of history."

Xavier gazed beyond his foster father up to the faint stars glimmering through the dusk. He could identify some of those stars, and knew which systems were controlled by Omnius, which were League Worlds.

"I will also learn how to fight the thinking machines," he said. Emil Tantor squeezed his shoulder. "I will defeat them one day."

It is my purpose in life.

XI

On a dark night in the bright snowfield and dark pines, the Caladan primitives sat on furs around a roaring fire. Keeping their oral tradition alive, they repeated the ancient legends and stories of recent battles. The elder Tiddoc sat beside the foreigner accepted among them, a hero with bright eyes and waxy, horribly scarred skin. A man who had fought single-handedly against a cymek monster and fallen into a scalding hot opening … but had crawled out alive, clinging to the battered cymek walker-form.

Piers gestured with one hand; the other—burned and twisted into uselessness—hung limp against his chest. He spoke passionately in the ancient Buddislamic tongue, halting as he struggled for words and then continuing when Tiddoc helped him.

Caladan was his home now, and he would live the rest of his life with these people, in obscurity. No escape seemed possible from such a remote place, except through the stories he told. Piers kept his audience enthralled as he spoke of great battles against the thinking machines, while he also learned the Songs of the Long Trek, chronicles of the many generations of Zensunni Wanderings.

As his father had realized, Piers Harkonnen had always wanted to be a storyteller.

Whipping Mek

Introduction

Our second Jihad-era story, "Whipping Mek," bridges the first and second novels in the trilogy, *The Butlerian Jihad* and *The Machine Crusade*. The story is set at a vital point in the nearly quarter-century gap between the events in these two novels, and fleshes out a pair of key tragic figures from later parts of the story.

Tor Books released this story as a free booklet distributed widely in bookstores across the US, and many copies included a bonus CD that included an audio version of the story, read by Scott Brick.

Whipping Mek

When the armored Jihad warship arrived, the population of Giedi Prime expected news of a great victory against the evil thinking machines. But with only a glance at the battle-scarred vessel, young Vergyl Tantor could tell that the defense of Peridot Colony had not gone at all as planned.

On the crowded fringe of Giedi City Spaceport, Vergyl rushed forward, pressing against the soldiers stuck there as ground troops, like himself: wide-eyed green recruits or veterans too old to be sent into battle against Omnius's combat robots. His heart hammered like an industrial piston in his chest.

He prayed that his adoptive brother, Xavier Harkonnen, was all right.

The damaged battleship heaved itself into the docking circle like a dying sea beast beached on a reef. The big engines hissed and groaned as they cooled from the hot descent through the atmosphere.

Vergyl stared at the blackened scars on the hull plates and tried to imagine the kinetic weapons and high-energy projectiles that combat robots had inflicted upon the brave Jihadi defenders.

If only he had been out there himself, Vergyl could have helped in the fight. But Xavier—the commander of the battle group—always seemed to fight against his brother's eagerness with nearly as much persistence as he fought against the machine enemy.

When the landing systems finished locking down, dozens of egress hatches opened on the lower hull. Middle-ranking Jihad commanders emerged, bellowing for assistance. All medically qualified personnel were called in from the city; others were shuttled from across the continents of Giedi Prime to help the wounded soldiers and rescued colonists.

Triage and assessment stations were set up on the spaceport grounds. Official military personnel were tended first, since they had pledged their lives to fight in the great struggle ignited by Serena Butler. Their crimson-and-green uniforms were stained and badly patched; they'd obviously had no chance to repair them during the many weeks of transit from Peridot Colony. Mercenary soldiers received second-priority treatment, along with the refugees from the colony.

Vergyl rushed in with the other ground-based soldiers to help, his large brown eyes flicking back and forth in search of answers. He needed to find someone who could tell him what had happened to Segundo Harkonnen. Worry scratched at Vergyl's mind while he worked. Perhaps everything was all right … but what if his big brother had been killed in a heroic rally? Or what if he was injured, yet remained aboard the battered ship, refusing to accept help for himself until all of his personnel were tended to? Both of those scenarios would have fit Xavier's personality.

For hours, Vergyl refused to slow down, unable to fully grasp what these Jihadi fighters had been through. Sweating and exhausted, he worked himself into a trancelike stupor, following orders, helping one after another of the wounded, burned, and despairing refugees.

He heard muttered conversations that told of the onslaught that had wiped out the small colony. When the thinking machines had attempted to absorb the settlement into the Synchronized Worlds, the Army of the Jihad had sent its defenders there.

Peridot Colony had been but a skirmish, however, like so many others in the dozen years since Serena Butler had originally rallied all humans to fight in her cause, after the thinking machines murdered her young son, Manion. *Xavier's son.*

The ebb and flow of the Jihad had caused a great deal of damage to both sides, but neither fighting force had gained a clear upper hand. And though the thinking machines continued to build fresh combat robots, lost human lives could never be replaced. Serena gave passionate speeches to recruit new soldiers for her holy war. So many fighters had died that the Jihad no longer publicly revealed the cost. The struggle was everything.

Following the Honru Massacre seven years earlier, Vergyl had insisted on joining the Army of the Jihad himself. He considered it his duty as a human being, even without his connection to Xavier and the martyred child, Manion. At their estate on Salusa Secundus, his parents had tried to make the young man wait, since he was barely seventeen, but Vergyl would hear none of it.

Returning to Salusa after a difficult skirmish, Xavier had surprised their parents by offering a waiver that would allow underage Vergyl to begin training in the Army. The young man had leaped at the opportunity, not guessing that Xavier had his own plans. Overprotective, Segundo Harkonnen had seen to it that Vergyl received a safe, quiet assignment, stationed here on Giedi Prime where he could help with the rebuilding work—and where he would stay far from any pitched battles against the robotic enemy.

Now Vergyl had been in Giedi City for years, rising minimally in rank to second decero in the Construction Brigade … never seeing any action. Meanwhile, Xavier Harkonnen's battleships went to planet after planet, protecting free humanity and destroying the mechanized legions of the computer evermind Omnius ….

Vergyl stopped counting all the bodies he'd moved. Perspiring in his dark-green uniform, the young construction officer and a civilian man carried a makeshift stretcher, hauling a wounded mother who had been rescued from her devastated prefab home on Peridot Colony. Women and children from Giedi City hurried among the workers and wounded, offering water and food.

Finally, in the warm afternoon, a ragged cheer penetrated Vergyl's dazed focus, as he set the stretcher down in the midst of a triage unit. Looking up, he drew in a quick breath. At the warship's main entrance ramp, a proud military commander stepped forward into the sunshine of Giedi Prime.

Xavier Harkonnen wore a clean segundo's uniform with immaculate golden insignia. By careful design, he cut a dashing military figure, one that would inspire confidence and faith among his own troops as well as the civilians of Giedi City. Fear was the worst enemy the machines could bring against them. Xavier never offered any observer reason for uncertainty: Yes, brave humanity would eventually win this war.

Grinning, Vergyl let out a sigh as all his doubts evaporated. Of course Xavier had survived. This great man had led the strike force that liberated Giedi Prime from the enslavement of cymeks and thinking machines. Xavier had commanded the human forces in the atomic purification of Earth, the first great battle of Serena Butler's Jihad.

And the heroic Segundo Xavier Harkonnen would never stop until the thinking machines were defeated.

But as Vergyl watched his brother walk down the ramp, he noticed that the brave commander's footsteps had a heavy, weary quality, and his familiar face looked shell-shocked. Not even a hint of a smile there, no gleam in his gray eyes. Just flat stoniness. How had the man gotten so old? Vergyl idolized him, needed to speak with him alone as a brother, so that he could learn the real story.

But in public, Segundo Harkonnen would never let anyone see his inner feelings. He was too good a leader for that.

Vergyl pushed his way through the throng, shouting and waving with the others, and finally Xavier recognized him in the sea of faces. His expression lit with joy, then crashed, as if weighed down by the burden of war memories and realizations. Vergyl and his fellow relief workers hurried up the ramp to surround the lead officer and escorted him into the safety of Giedi City.

✧ ✧ ✧

Along with his surviving sub-commanders, Xavier Harkonnen spent hours dispensing reports and debriefing League officials, but he insisted on breaking away from these painful duties to spend a few hours with his brother.

He arrived at Vergyl's small home unrested, eyes bloodshot and haunted. When the two of them hugged, Xavier remained stiff for a moment, before weakening and returning his dark-skinned brother's embrace. Despite the physical dissimilarities that marked their separate racial heritage, they knew that the bonds of love had nothing to do with bloodlines and everything to do with the loving family experiences they had shared in the household of Emil and Lucille Tantor. Leading him inside, Vergyl could sense the tremors Xavier was suppressing. He distracted Xavier by introducing him to his wife of two years, whom Xavier had never met.

Sheel was a young, dark-haired beauty not accustomed to receiving guests of such importance. She had not even traveled to Salusa Secundus to meet Vergyl's parents or to see the Tantor family estate. But she treated Xavier as her husband's welcome brother, instead of as a celebrity.

One of Aurelius Venport's merchant ships had arrived only a week before, carrying melange from Arrakis. Sheel had gone out this afternoon and spent a week's pay to get enough of the expensive spice to add to the fine, special dinner she prepared.

As they ate, their conversation remained subdued and casual, avoiding any mention of war news. Weary to the bone, Xavier seemed barely to notice the flavors of the meal, even the exotic melange. Sheel seemed disappointed, until Vergyl explained in a whisper that his brother had lost much of his sense of taste and smell during a cymek gas attack, which had also cost him his lungs. Although Xavier now breathed through a set of replacement organs provided by a Tlulaxa flesh merchant, his ability to taste or smell remained dulled.

Finally, as they drank spice-laced coffee, Vergyl could no longer withhold his questions. "Xavier, please tell me what happened at Peridot Colony. Was it a victory, or did the—" his voice caught "—did the machines defeat us?"

Xavier lifted his head, looking far away. "Grand Patriarch Iblis Ginjo says that there are no defeats. Only victories and … moral victories. This one fell into the latter category."

Sheel squeezed her husband's arm sharply, a wordless request that he withdraw the question. But Vergyl didn't interrupt, and Xavier continued, "Peridot Colony had been under attack for a week before our nearest battle group received the emergency distress call. Settlers were being obliterated. The thinking machines meant to crush the colony and establish a Synchronized World there, to lay down their infrastructure and install a new copy of the Omnius evermind."

Xavier sipped spice coffee, while Vergyl put his elbows on the table, leaning close to listen with rapt attention.

"The Army of the Jihad had little presence in this area aside from my warship and a handful of troops. We had no choice but to respond, not wishing to lose another planet. I had a full shipload of mercenaries anyway."

"Any from Ginaz? Our best fighters?"

"Some. We arrived faster than the thinking machines expected, struck them swiftly and mercilessly, using everything we had. My mercenaries attacked like madmen, and many of them fell. But a lot more thinking machines were destroyed. Unfortunately, most of the colony towns had already been trampled by the time we got there, the inhabitants murdered. Even so, our Army of the Jihad drove in—and by a holy miracle we pushed back the enemy forces." He drew a deep, convulsing breath, as if his replacement lungs were malfunctioning.

"Instead of simply cutting their losses and flying away, as combat robots usually do, this time they were programmed to follow a scorched-earth policy. They devastated everything in their wake. Where they had gone, not a crop, structure, or human survivor was left behind."

Sheel swallowed hard. "How terrible."

"*Terrible?*" Xavier mused, rolling the sound of the word on his tongue. "I cannot begin to describe what I saw. Not much was left of the colony we went to rescue. Over a quarter of my Jihadi fighters lost their lives, and half of the mercenaries."

Shaking his head sadly, he continued. "We scraped together the pathetic remnants of settlers who had fled far enough from the primary machine forces. I do not know—nor do I want to know—the actual number of survivors we rescued. Peridot Colony did not fall to the machines, but that world is no longer of any use to humans, either." He heaved a deep breath. "It seems to be the way of this Jihad."

"That is why we need to keep fighting." Vergyl lifted his chin. His bravery sounded tinny in his own ears. "Let me fight at your side against Omnius! The Army of the Jihad is in constant need of soldiers. It's time for me to get into the real battles in this war!"

Now Xavier Harkonnen seemed to awaken. Dismay flashed across his face. "You don't want that, Vergyl. Not *ever*."

⌂ ⌂ ⌂

Vergyl secured an assignment working aboard the Jihad warship as it underwent repairs for the better part of two weeks. If he couldn't fly off and fight on alien battlefields, at least he could be here recharging weapons, replacing damaged Holtzman shield systems, and strengthening armor plating.

While Vergyl diligently performed every task the team supervisors assigned to him, his eyes drank in details about how the ship's systems functioned. Someday, if Xavier ever relented and allowed him to participate in the Holy Jihad, Vergyl wanted to command one of these vessels. He was an adult—twenty-three years old—but his influential brother had the power to interfere with anything he tried to do … and had already done so.

That afternoon, as he checked off the progress of repairs on his display pad, Vergyl came upon one of the battleship's training chambers. The dull metal door stood half open, and he heard a clattering and clanging of metal, and the grunting sounds of someone straining with great effort.

Rushing into the chamber, Vergyl stopped and stared in astonishment. A long-haired, battle-scarred man—a mercenary, judging from his wild, disheveled appearance—threw himself in violent combat against a fighting robot. The machine had three sets of articulated arms, each one holding a deadly-looking weapon. Moving in a graceful blur, the mechanical unit struck blow after blow against the man, who defended himself perfectly each time.

Vergyl's heart leaped. How had one of the enemy machines gotten on board Xavier's battleship? Had Omnius sent it as a spy or saboteur? Were there others spread out around the ship? The beleaguered mercenary landed a blow with his vibrating pulse sword, causing one of the mek's six arms to drop limply to its side.

Letting out a war cry, knowing he had to help, Vergyl snatched the only weapon he could find—a training staff from a rack by the wall—and charged forward recklessly.

The mercenary reacted quickly upon hearing Vergyl's approach. He raised a hand. "Hold, Chirox!"

The combat mek froze. The mercenary, panting, dropped his fighting stance. Vergyl skidded to a halt, looking in confusion from the enemy robot to the well-muscled fighter.

"Don't alarm yourself," the mercenary said. "I was simply practicing."

"With a *machine?*"

The long-haired man smiled. A spiderweb of pale scars covered his cheeks, neck, bare shoulders, and chest. "Thinking machines are our enemies in this Jihad, young officer. If we must develop our skills against them, who better to fight?"

Awkwardly, Vergyl set his hastily grabbed staff on the deck. His face flushed hot with embarrassment. "That makes sense."

"Chirox is just a surrogate enemy, a target to fight. He represents all thinking machines in my mind."

"Like a whipping boy."

"A whipping mek." The mercenary smiled. "We can set it to various fighting levels for training purposes." He stepped closer to the ominous-looking combat robot. "Stand down."

The robot lowered its weapons-studded limbs, then retracted them into its core, even the impaired arm, and stood waiting for further commands. With a sneer, the man slammed the hilt of his pulse sword against the mek's chest, knocking the mek backward a step. The optic-sensor eyes flickered orange. The rest of the machine's face, with its crudely shaped mouth and nose, did not move.

Confidently, the man tapped the metallic torso. "This limited robot—I dislike the term *thinking machine*—is totally under our control. It has served the mercenaries of Ginaz for nearly three generations now." He deactivated his pulse sword, which was designed to scramble the sophisticated gelcircuitry of a thinking machine. "I am Zon Noret, one of the fighters assigned to this ship."

Intrigued, Vergyl ventured closer. "Where did you find this machine?"

"A century ago, a Ginaz salvage scout found a damaged thinking-machine ship, from which he retrieved this broken combat robot. Since then, we've wiped its memories and reinstalled combat programming. It allows us to test ourselves against machine capabilities."

Noret patted the robot on one of its ribbed metal shoulders. "Many robots in the Synchronized Worlds have been destroyed because of what we learned from this unit. Chirox is an invaluable teacher. On the archipelago of Ginaz, students pit their skills against him. He has proved to be such an advantage and a repository of information to utilize against our enemy that we mercenaries no longer refer to him as a thinking machine, but as an ally."

"A robot as an ally? Serena Butler wouldn't like to hear that," Vergyl said guardedly.

Zon Noret tossed his thick hair behind his head like the mane of a comet. "Many things are done in this Jihad without Serena Butler knowing. I wouldn't be surprised to learn of other meks like this one under our control." He made a dismissive gesture. "But since we all have the same goal, the details become insignificant."

To Vergyl, some of Noret's wounds looked only freshly healed. "Shouldn't you be recuperating from the battle, instead of fighting even more?"

"A true mercenary never stops fighting." His eyes narrowed. "I see you're an officer yourself."

Vergyl let out a frustrated sigh. "In the Construction Brigade. It's not what I wanted. I wanted to fight, but … it's a long story."

Noret wiped sweat from his brow. "Your name?"

"Second Decero Tantor."

With no flicker of recognition at the name, Noret looked at the combat mek and then at the young officer. "Perhaps we can arrange a little taste of battle for you anyway."

"You would let me …?" Vergyl felt his pulse quicken.

Zon Noret nodded. "If a man wants to fight, he should be allowed to do so."

Vergyl lifted his chin. "I couldn't agree more."

"I warn you, this may be a training mek, but it is lethal. I often disconnect its safety protocol during my rigorous practices. That is why Ginaz mercenaries are so good."

"There must be fail-safes, otherwise it wouldn't be much good as an instructor."

"Training that entails no risk is not realistic. It makes the student soft, knowing he is in no danger. Chirox is not like that, by design. It could kill you."

Vergyl felt a rush of bravado, hoped he wasn't being foolish. "I can handle myself. I've gone through Jihad training of my own." But he wanted a chance to prove himself, and this combat robot might be as close to the fight as he ever got. Vergyl focused his hatred on Chirox, thought of all the horrors the fighting machines had inflicted upon humanity, and wanted to smash the mek into scrap metal. "Let me fight it, just as you were doing."

The mercenary raised his eyebrows, as if amused and interested. "Your choice of weapons, young warrior?"

Vergyl fumbled, looked at the clumsy training staff he had grabbed. "I didn't bring anything but this."

Noret held his pulse sword up for the younger man to examine. "Do you know how to operate one of these?"

"That looks like one we used in basic training, but a newer model."

"Correct." Noret activated the weapon and handed it to the young man.

Vergyl hefted the sword to check its balance. Shimmering arcs of disruptive energy ran along the surface of its blade.

He took a deep breath and studied the combat mek, who stared back at him dispassionately, its eyelike optic sensors glowing orange … waiting. The sensors shifted direction, watched Noret approach and prepared for another opponent.

When the mercenary activated the mek, only two of the six mechanical arms emerged from the torso. One metal hand clasped a dagger, while the other was empty.

"It's fighting me at a low difficulty setting," Vergyl complained.

"Perhaps Chirox is just testing you. In actual combat, your adversary will never provide a résumé of his skills beforehand."

Vergyl moved carefully toward the mek, then shifted to his left and circled, holding the pulse sword. He felt moisture on his palm, loosened his grip a bit. The mek kept turning to face him. Its dagger hand twitched, and Vergyl jabbed at the robot's weapon with the electronic sword, hitting it with a purple pulse that caused the robot to shudder.

"Looks like a dumb machine to me." He had imagined combat like this. Vergyl darted toward his opponent and struck the torso with the pulse sword, leaving a purple discoloration on the metal body. He tapped a blue button on the weapon's handle until it reached the highest pulse setting.

"Go for the head," Noret counseled. "Scramble the robot's circuits to slow him. If you strike Chirox just right, he will need a minute or two to reconfigure."

Again Vergyl struck, but missed the head, sliding down to the armored shoulder. Multicolored sparks covered the mek's outer surface, and the dagger dropped from its mechanical grip to clatter on the floor of the training chamber. A wisp of smoke rose from the robot's hand.

Vergyl moved in for the kill. He didn't care if anyone needed this fighting unit for training. He wanted to destroy it, to burn it into molten remains. He thought of Serena, of little Manion, of all the humans slaughtered … and of his own inability to fight for the Jihad. This scapegoat mek would have to do for now.

But as he stepped forward, suddenly the flowmetal of the robot's free hand shifted, reshaping itself, to extrude a short sword with barbs on the blade. The other hand stopped sparking, and a matching weapon also formed there.

"Careful, young warrior. We wouldn't want the Army of the Jihad to lose your construction skills."

Feeling a surge of anger at the remark, Vergyl snapped, "I'm not afraid of this machine."

"Fear is not always unwise."

"Even against a stupid opponent? Chirox doesn't even know I'm ridiculing him, does he?"

"I am just a machine," the mek recited, his synthesized voice coming from a speakerpatch. Vergyl was taken aback, thinking he had caught just a hint of sarcasm in the robot's voice. Like a theatrical mask, his face did not change its expression.

"Chirox doesn't usually say much," Noret said, smiling. "Go ahead, pound him some more. But even I don't know all the surprises he might have in store."

Vergyl moved back to reassess his opponent. He studied the robot's optic sensors, which glowed a steady orange, focused on the pulse weapon.

Abruptly, Chirox lunged with the barbed short sword, exhibiting unexpected speed and agility. Vergyl tried to dodge the blow, but not quickly enough, and a shallow gash opened on one of his arms. He went into a floor roll to escape, then glanced at the wound as he leaped back to his feet.

"Not a bad move," Noret said, his tone casual, as if he didn't care whether the robot killed Vergyl. Killing was both sport and profession to him. Maybe it took a harsh mindset to be a mercenary for Ginaz, but Vergyl—endowed with no such harshness—worried that he had gotten into this situation on impulse and might be facing a challenge more difficult than he was ready for. The combat mek kept advancing with jerking, unpredictable speeds, sometimes lunging, sometimes with an astonishing fluidity of motion.

Vergyl darted from side to side, striking blows with the pulse sword. He executed proficient rolls and considered attempting a showy backflip, but didn't know if he could pull it off. Failure to properly execute a move could prove fatal.

One of his pulse blows struck the panel box on Chirox's side, making it glow red. The robot paused. A thin, agile arm emerged from the robot's torso and adjusted something inside.

"It can repair itself?"

"Most combat meks can. You wanted a fair shot at a real machine opponent, didn't you? I warned you, this robot does not fight below its abilities."

Suddenly Chirox came at Vergyl harder and faster than before. Two more arms extruded from the body core. One held a long dagger with a jagged tip for snagging and ripping flesh. The other held a shimmering branding iron.

Zon Noret said something in an anxious tone, but the words blurred. The entire universe that Vergyl had known up to this point faded, along with all unnecessary sensory perception. He focused only on survival.

"I am a Jihadi," Vergyl whispered. He resigned himself to fate and at the same time decided to inflict as much damage as he could.

He recalled a pledge that even the Construction Brigade had to memorize: "If I die in battle against the machines, I will join those who have gone to Paradise before me, and those who follow." He felt a near-trancelike state consume him and remove all fear of death.

He plunged into battle, flailing away, striking the pulse sword against the mek, discharging the weapon repeatedly. In the background, someone shouted something, words he couldn't make out. Then Vergyl heard a loud click, saw a flash of color, and bright yellow light immersed him. It felt like a blast from a polar wind and froze him in place.

Immobilized, helpless, Vergyl shuddered, then toppled. He fell for what seemed like a great distance. His teeth chattered, and he shivered. He didn't seem to land anywhere.

Finally he found himself looking up into the robot's gleaming optic sensors. Totally vulnerable. "I can kill you now." The machine pressed the jagged tip of the long dagger against Vergyl's neck.

The combat mek could thrust the blade through his throat in a microsecond. Vergyl heard shouts, but could not squirm away. He stared up into the implacable optical sensors of the robot, the face of the hated machine enemy. The thinking machine was going to kill him—and this wasn't even a real battle. What a fool he had been.

Somewhere in the distance, familiar voices—two of them?—called out to him. "Vergyl! Vergyl! Shut the damn thing off, Noret!"

He tried to lift his head and look around, but could not move. Chirox continued to press the sharp point against his jugular vein. His muscles were paralyzed, as if frozen inside a block of ice.

"Get me a disruptor gun!" He recognized the voice at last. Xavier. Somehow, incongruously, Vergyl worried more about his brother's disapproval than dying.

But then the mek straightened and removed the dagger blade from his throat.

He heard more voices, the thumping of boots, and the clattering of weaponry. Peripherally, Vergyl saw movement, and the crimson-and-green of Jihadi uniforms. Xavier shouted commands to his men, but Chirox retracted the jagged dagger, its other weapons, and all four arms into its torso. The fiercely glowing optic sensors dulled to a soft glimmer.

Zon Noret placed himself in front of the robot. "Don't shoot, Segundo. Chirox could have killed him, but didn't. His programming is to take advantage of a weakness and deliver a mortal blow, yet he made a conscious decision against it."

"I did not wish to kill him." The combat robot reset itself to a stationary position. "It was not necessary."

Vergyl finally cleared his head enough to push himself into a stiff sitting position. "That mek actually showed … compassion." He still felt dazed from the mysterious stun blast. "Imagine that, a machine with feelings."

"It wasn't compassion at all," Xavier said, with a contentious scowl. He reached down to help his brother to his feet.

"It was the strangest thing," Vergyl insisted. "Did you see his eyes?"

Zon Noret, intent on his training mek, looked into the machine's panel box, studied instrument readings and made adjustments. "Chirox simply assessed the situation and went into survival mode. But there must have been something buried in his original programming."

"Machines don't care about survival," Xavier snapped. "You saw them at Peridot Colony. They hurl themselves into battle without concern for personal safety." He shook his head. "There's something wrong with your mek's programming, a glitch."

Vergyl stared over at Chirox, caught the gaze of the glowing optic sensors. In the depths of the twin lights, the young construction officer thought he detected a flicker of something animate, which intrigued and frightened him at the same time.

"Humans can learn compassion, too," Chirox said, unexpectedly.

"I'll run it through a complete overhaul," Noret said, but his voice was uncertain.

Xavier stood in front of Vergyl, checking his brother for serious injuries. He spoke in a shaky voice as he led his brother out of the training chamber. "That was quite a scare you gave me."

"I just wanted to fight … a real enemy for once."

Xavier looked deeply saddened. "Vergyl, I fear that you will have your chance, eventually. This Jihad will not be over anytime soon."

The Faces of a Martyr

Introduction

An even longer time passes between the second and third novels of the Butlerian Jihad trilogy, decades in which remarkable changes take place in the long war against the thinking machines. In our final bridging short story, "The Faces of a Martyr," the surviving main characters have altered dramatically, and we had a chance to portray the driving events that set up the final battle between the human race and their mortal enemies, the thinking machines, in *The Battle of Corrin.*

The Faces of a Martyr

"I'm sorry," Rekur Van said to his fellow Tlulaxa researcher as he slipped the knife deftly through the victim's spine, then added an extra twist. "I need this ship more than you do."

Blood seeped around the slender steel blade, then spilled in a final dying gush as Van yanked the knife back out. His comrade jittered and twitched as nerve endings attempted to fire. Van tumbled him out the hatch of the small vessel, discarding him onto the pavement of the spaceport.

Explosions, shouts, and weapons fire rang through the streets of the main Tlulaxa city. The fatally wounded genetic scientist sprawled on the ground, still shuddering, his close-set eyes dimming as they blinked accusations at Rekur Van. Discarded, like so many other vital things ….

He wiped the blood on his garments, but his hands remained sticky. He would have time to launder the clothes and clean his skin, once he escaped. Blood … it was the currency of his trade, a genetic resource filled with useful DNA. He hated to waste so much of it.

But now the League of Nobles wanted blood. *His* blood.

Though he was one of the most brilliant Tlulaxa scientists and well connected with powerful religious leaders, Van had to flee his homeworld to escape the lynch mobs. Outraged members of the League blockaded the planet and swept in to exact their justice. If they caught him, he could not begin to imagine the retribution they would inflict upon him. "Fanatics—all of you!" he shouted uselessly toward the city, then sealed the hatch.

With no time to retrieve his priceless research documents and forced to leave his personal wealth behind, Van used his blood-stained hands to operate the stolen ship's controls. Without a plan, wanting only to get off the planet before the vengeful League soldiers could seize him, he launched his vessel into the sky.

"Damn you, Iblis Ginjo!" he said to himself. It gave him very little consolation to know that the Grand Patriarch was already dead.

Ginjo had always treated him as a lower form of life. Van and the Grand Patriarch had been business associates who depended on each other but shared no feelings of trust. In the end, the League had discovered the horrific secret of the Tlulaxa organ farms: missing soldiers and Zensunni slaves were cut up to provide replacement parts for other wounded fighters. Now the tables had turned. All of the Tlulaxa were in turmoil, scrambling for their lives to escape the League's indignant vengeance. Flesh merchants had to go into hiding, and legitimate traders were run off of civilized worlds. Disgraced and ruined, Van was now a hunted man.

But even without his laboratory records, his mind still carried vital knowledge to be shared with the highest bidder. And sealed in a pocket he took with him a small vial of special genetic material that would allow him to start over again. If he could only get away …

Reaching orbit in his stolen ship, Van saw powerful javelin battleships manned by angry Jihadis. Numerous Tlulaxa vessels—most of them flown by inexperienced and panicked pilots such as himself—streaked away in a pell-mell fashion, and the League warships targeted all Tlulaxa craft that came within range.

"Why not just assume we're *all* guilty?" he snarled at the images, knowing no one could hear him.

Van increased acceleration, not knowing how fast the unfamiliar ship could go. With the end of his sleeve, he wiped away a blot of drying blood on the control panel so he could read the instruments better. The League javelins took potshots at him, and an angry voice came over the commline.

"Tlulaxa craft! Stand down—surrender or be destroyed."

"Why not use your weapons against the thinking machines?" Van retorted. "The Army of the Jihad is wasting time and resources here. Or have you forgotten the real enemies of humanity?" Surely any supposed Tlulaxa crimes were minimal compared to decades of devastation by the computer evermind Omnius.

Apparently, the javelin commander did not appreciate his sarcasm. Exploding projectiles streaked silently past him, and Van reacted with a sudden lurch of deceleration; the artillery detonated some distance from its intended target, but the shock wave still put his stolen ship into a spin. Flashing lights and alarm signals lit the control panels in the cockpit, but Van did not send out a distress signal. Noiselessly, he tumbled out of control, playing dead—and the League ships soon left him to hunt other hapless Tlulaxa escapees. They had plenty of victims to choose from.

When the League battleships were finally gone, Van felt he was safe enough to engage stabilizers. After several exaggerated attempts, he compensated for the out-of-control rolling and got his ship back on course. With no destination in mind, intent only on escaping, he flew out of the system as far and as fast as he could go. He did not regret what he was leaving behind.

For most of his life, Van had worked to develop vital new biological techniques, as had generations of his people before him. During the Jihad, the Tlulaxa had made themselves fabulously wealthy, and presumably indispensable. Now, though, Serena's fanatics would raze the original organ farms, destroying the transplant tanks, and "mercifully" putting the donors out of their misery. Short-sighted fools! How the League would complain in coming years when eyeless or limbless veterans wailed about their injuries and had nowhere else to go.

The myopic League idealists didn't consider practical matters, didn't plan well at all. As with so many things in Serena Butler's Jihad, they chased unrealistic dreams, were driven by foolish emotions. Van hated those people.

He grasped the ship's control bar as if to strangle it, pretending it was Iblis Ginjo's thick neck. Despite a full résumé of despicable acts, the Grand Patriarch had succeeded in keeping his own name clean while shifting blame onto an old, hard-bitten war hero, Xavier Harkonnen, and the whole Tlulaxa race. Ginjo's ever-scheming widow falsely portrayed her fallen husband as a martyr.

The League could steal the "honor" of the Tlulaxa people. Mobs could take their wealth and force his people to live as outlaws. But the betrayers could never take away Rekur Van's special knowledge and skills. This scapegoat was still able to fight back.

Finally, Van made up his mind where he should go, where he should take his secret and innovative cloning technology, as well as viable cells from Serena Butler herself.

He headed out past the boundaries of League space to find the machine worlds, where he intended to present himself to the ever-mind Omnius.

✡ ✡ ✡

On Salusa Secundus, capital of the League of Nobles, a screaming, unruly crowd set fire to the figure of a man.

Stony silent, Vorian Atreides stood in the shadows of an ornate arch, watching the crowd. His throat was clenched so tightly that he could not shout his dismay. Though he was a champion of the Jihad, this wild throng would not listen to him.

The effigy was a poor likeness of Xavier Harkonnen, but the mob's hatred for him was unmistakable. The mannequin dangled from a makeshift gibbet above a pile of dry sticks. A young man tossed in a small igniter, and within seconds outstretched flames began to consume the effigy's symbolic Army of the Jihad uniform—like the one Xavier had been so proud to wear.

Vorian's friend had devoted most of his life to the war against the thinking machines. Now an irrational throng had found a uniform and used it to mock him, stripping it of all medals and insignia, in much the same way Xavier had been stripped of his rightful place in history. Now they were burning him.

As the fire caught, the figure danced and smoldered on the end of its tether. Raucous cheering rattled the windows of nearby buildings, celebrating the death of a traitor. The people considered this an act of vengeance. Vor considered it an abomination.

After Vor learned how brave Xavier had exposed the Tlulaxa organ farms and brought down the treacherous Grand Patriarch Ginjo, he had rushed to Salusa. He'd never expected to witness such an appalling and well-orchestrated backlash against his friend. For days Vor had continued to speak out, trying to stop the hysterical anger from striking the wrong target. Despite his high rank, few came to his support. The smear campaign against Xavier had begun, and history was being rewritten even while it was still news. Vor felt like a man standing on the beach in a Caladan hurricane, holding up his hands to ward off a tidal wave.

Even Xavier's own daughters bowed to pressure and changed their names from Harkonnen to their mother's surname of Butler. Their mother Octa, always quiet and shy, had withdrawn in misery to the City of Introspection, refusing to see outsiders ….

Wearing street clothes to conceal his identity, Vor stood among the crowd, unnoticed. Like Xavier, he was proud of his service in the Army of the Jihad, but in the mounting emotional fervor this was no time to appear in uniform.

Over the course of the long Jihad, Primero Vorian Atreides had engaged in many battles against the thinking machines. He had fought at Xavier's side and achieved tremendous, but costly, victories. Xavier was the bravest man Vor had ever known, and now billions of people despised him.

Unable to tolerate the spectacle any longer, Vor turned away from the throng. Such mass ignorance and stupidity! The ill-informed and easily manipulated multitude would believe whatever they chose to. Vorian Atreides alone would remember the brave truth about the Harkonnen name.

✿ ✿ ✿

The independent robot stepped back to admire the new sign mounted on his laboratory wall. *Understanding human nature is the most difficult of all mental exercises.*

While considering the implications of the statement, Erasmus shifted the expression on his flowmetal face. For centuries his quest had been to decipher these biological creatures: They had so many flaws, but somehow, in a spark of genius, they had created thinking machines. The puzzle intrigued him.

He had mounted various slogans around his laboratory to initiate trains of thought at unexpected times. Philosophy was far more than a game to him; it was a means by which he improved his machine mind.

It Is Possible to Achieve Whatever You Envision, Whether You Are Man or Machine.

To facilitate his better understanding of the biological enemy, Erasmus performed constant experiments. Strapped onto tables, confined within transparent tanks, or sealed within airtight cells, the robot's current round of subjects moaned and writhed. Some prayed to invisible gods. Others screamed and begged for mercy from their captor, which showed just how delusional they were. A number bled, urinated, and leaked all manner of fluids, discourteously messing his laboratory. Fortunately, he had subservient robots as well as human slaves to restore the facility to an antiseptic and orderly state.

Flesh Is Just Soft Metal.

The robot had dissected thousands of human brains and bodies, in addition to conducting psychological experiments. He tested people with sensory deprivation, causing extreme pain and unrelenting fear. He studied the behavior of individuals as well as crowd activities. Yet through it all, despite his meticulous attention to detail, Erasmus knew he continued to miss something important. He could not find a way to assess and collate all the data so that it fit within a comprehensible framework, a "grand unified theory" of human nature. The behavioral extremes were too far separated.

Is It More Human to Be Good? Or Evil?

That sign, next to the new one, had posed a conundrum for some time. Many of the humans he had studied in detail, such as Serena Butler and his own ward Gilbertus Albans, demonstrated an innate human goodness filled with compassion and caring for other creatures. But Erasmus had studied history and knew about traitors and sociopaths who caused incredible damage and suffering in order to gain advantages for themselves.

No set of conclusions made sense.

After thirty-six years of Serena Butler's Jihad, the machines were far from victory, despite computer projections that said they should have crushed the feral humans long ago. Fanaticism kept the League of Nobles strong, and they continued to fight when any reasoned consideration should have led them to surrender. Their inspirational leader had been martyred … by her own choice. An inexplicable act.

Now, he finally had a fresh opportunity, an unexpected new subject that might shed light on hitherto unexplored aspects of humanity. Perhaps when he arrived, the Tlulaxa captive would provide some answers. After all, the foolish man had fallen into their laps ….

Rekur Van had brashly flown into Synchronized space controlled by the thinking machines, and transmitted his demand to see Omnius. The Tlulaxa's bold arrival was either part of a complicated trick … or he genuinely believed he had a worthwhile bargaining chip. Erasmus was curious as to which it was.

Omnius wanted to destroy the Tlulaxa ship outright; most humans trespassing in Synchronized space were either killed or captured, but Erasmus intervened, eager to hear what the well-known genetics researcher had to say.

After surrounding the small vessel, robotic warships escorted it to Corrin, center of the Synchronized Worlds. Without delay, armored sentinel robots marched the captive directly into Erasmus's laboratory.

Rekur Van's angular, gray-skinned face was pinched into a scowl that flickered between haughtiness and fear. His dark, close-set eyes blinked rapidly. He wore a braid down to his shoulder and tried to look confident and nonplused, but failed completely.

Facing him, the autonomous robot preened in his plush, regal robe, which he wore to make himself impressive in the eyes of his human slaves and test subjects. He fashioned a nonthreatening smile on his flowmetal face, then glowered, trying out another expression. "When you were captured, you demanded to see Omnius. It is strange for the great computer evermind to receive commands from such a diminutive human—a man both small in stature and in importance."

Van lifted his chin and sniffed haughtily. "You underestimate me." Reaching into the folds of his stained and rumpled tunic, the Tlulaxa withdrew a small vial. "I have brought you something precious. These are samples of vital cells, the raw materials of my genetic research."

"I have done a great deal of my own research," Erasmus said. "And I have many samples to draw from. Why should yours interest me?"

"Because these are original cells from *Serena Butler* herself. And you have no technology or techniques to grow an accelerated clone of her, as I do. I can create a perfect duplicate of the leader of the Jihad against thinking machines—I'm sure you can think of a use for that."

Erasmus was indeed impressed. "Serena Butler? You can recreate her?"

"Down to her exact DNA, and I can accelerate her maturity to whatever point you wish. But I have planted certain … inhibitors … in these cells. Little locks that only I can open." He continued to hold the vial tantalizingly in the laboratory's light, where Erasmus could see it. "Just imagine how valuable such a pawn could be in your war against humans."

"And why would you offer us such a treasure?"

"Because I hate the League of Nobles. They turned against my people, are hunting us down at every turn. If the thinking machines grant me sanctuary, I will reward you with a brand-new Serena Butler, to do with as you wish."

Possibilities flooded Erasmus's mental core. Serena had been his most fascinating human subject ever, but his experiments and tests on her had come to a grinding halt once he'd killed her unruly baby. After that, she was no longer cooperative. For decades, the robot had wished for a second opportunity with her—and now he could have it.

He imagined the dialogues they might have, the exchanges of ideas, the *answers* to all his pressing questions. He studied another slogan on the wall. *If I Can Think of the Ultimate Question, Will It Have an Answer?*

Fascinated, Erasmus clasped Van's shoulder, causing the Tlulaxa to grimace in pain. "I agree to your terms."

✿ ✿ ✿

The Grand Patriarch's widow sent him a formal invitation, and Vorian Atreides knew it was not an idle request.

The message was delivered by a captain of the Jihad Police, which in itself carried an implied threat. But Vor chose not to be intimidated. He donned many of the medals, ribbons, and decorations he'd been awarded over the course of his long and illustrious career. Although he'd grown up among thinking machines as a trustee, Vor had later become a Hero of the Jihad. He didn't want Iblis Ginjo's pretentious wife to forget for one second who she was dealing with.

Camie Boro-Ginjo had married Ginjo for the prestige his name offered, but it had been a loveless union between loveless people. Camie had every intention of turning her husband's spectacular death to her own political gain. Now, inside the same offices where the Grand Patriarch had formulated so many of his nefarious schemes, she sat beside the bald, olive-skinned Jipol commandant, Yorek Thurr. Vor steeled himself for whatever this dangerous pair might be planning.

Smiling prettily, Camie directed Vor's attention to a model on a display platform, a small-scale rendition of a grandiose monument. "This will be our shrine to the Three Martyrs. Anyone who glimpses it cannot help but be filled with fervor for the Jihad."

Vor eyed the arches, the huge braziers to carry eternal flames, and the three colossal figures inside, stylized representations of a man, woman, and child. "Three Martyrs?"

"Serena Butler and her child, murdered by the thinking machines, and my husband Iblis Ginjo, slain by the treachery of humans."

Vor could barely suppress his anger. He turned to leave. "I will have no part in this."

"Primero, please hear us out." Camie raised her hands in a placating gesture. "We must address the extreme turmoil in the League, the horrible murder of Serena Butler by the thinking machines, and the tragic death of my husband due to the plot hatched by Xavier Harkonnen and his Tlulaxa cohorts."

"There are no facts to prove Xavier's culpability," Vor said, his voice brittle. Camie had been primarily responsible for the blame-shifting and mudslinging. He was not afraid of her, or of her henchman. "Your assumptions are false, and you have stopped looking for the truth."

"It has been proven to my satisfaction."

Thurr rose to his feet. Though shorter in stature than Camie, he had the coiled strength of a cobra. "More to the point, Primero, it has been proven to the satisfaction of the League citizens. They need their heroes and martyrs."

"Apparently they need their villains as well. And, if you cannot find the correct culprit, you create one—as you did with Xavier."

Thurr meshed his fingers together. "We don't wish to engage in an acrimonious debate, Primero. You are a great military strategist, and we owe many of our victories to you."

"And to Xavier," Vor said.

The Jipol commandant continued without responding to the comment. "We three important leaders must work together to accomplish important goals. None of us can be mired down by bruised feelings and traditional grieving. We must keep the populace focused on winning our Holy Jihad, and cannot afford arguments that divert us from the real enemy. You persist in raising questions about what happened between Xavier Harkonnen and the Grand Patriarch, but you do not realize the damage you're doing."

"The truth is the truth."

"The truth is relative, and must be taken in the context of our larger struggle. Even Serena and Xavier would agree that unpleasant sacrifices are warranted if they help to achieve the goals of the Jihad. You must stop this personal crusade, Primero. Stop casting doubts. You only harm our cause if you don't keep your feelings to yourself."

Though Thurr's words were spoken calmly, Vor read the implied threat in them and suppressed a fleeting urge to strike the man; this Jipol commandant had no comprehension of honor or truth. No doubt, Thurr had the power to see that the Primero was quietly assassinated … and Vor knew he would do it if he considered it necessary.

Still, the Jipol commandant had struck a solid blow, reminding him of his friends' intentional sacrifices. If Vor destroyed the public confidence in the Jihad Council and the League government as a whole, the political repercussions and social turmoil could be considerable. Scandals, resignations, and the general uproar would severely weaken the solidarity the human race needed in order to face the thinking machines.

Omnius was the only enemy that mattered.

Vor crossed his arms over his heavily medaled and ribboned chest. "For now, I will keep my opinions to myself," he said. "But I don't do it for you and your power plays. I'm doing it for Serena's Jihad, and for Xavier."

"Just so long as you do it," Camie said.

Vor turned to leave, but paused at the door. "I don't want to be anywhere around when you unveil your Three Martyrs farce, so I'm heading for the front lines." Shaking his head, he hurried away. "Battles I can understand."

✿ ✿ ✿

On the main machine world of Corrin, years passed, and a female child grew rapidly into adulthood, her cloned life accelerated by Rekur Van. Erasmus regularly visited his laboratories full of moaning experimental subjects, where his new Serena Butler was taking shape nicely.

Among the tormented human subjects, the Tlulaxa researcher seemed quite at home. Van was himself an interesting person, with opinions and attitudes dramatically different from those Erasmus had observed in the original Serena or in Gilbertus Albans. Even so, the intense scientist had an unusual perspective: entirely self-centered, twisted by irrational hatred and spite toward the feral humans. In addition, he was intelligent and well trained. A good mental sparring partner for Erasmus … but the robot pinned his hopes on the return of Serena.

During her prolonged development, Van used advanced machine instructional technology to fill her head with misinformation, false memories mixed with details of the real Serena's life. Some of the data took hold; some of it needed to be implanted again and again.

When he had the opportunity, the robot engaged his new Serena in tentative conversation, anxious for the forthcoming days

69

when he could debate with her, provoking her ire and her fascinating responses—just as it had once been. But though she looked like an adult, Rekur Van insisted that the clone's preparation was not complete.

And after all this time, Erasmus was growing impatient.

At first, he had assumed the discrepancies from the Serena he had known were inconsequential, the difference between a juvenile and the woman she would ultimately become. But as the clone approached the equivalent age at which he had known Serena, Erasmus became increasingly disturbed. This wasn't at all what he had expected.

Sensing that he could no longer justify further delays, the Tlulaxa researcher rushed his final preparations. Dressed again in his regal robe, Erasmus arrived to observe as the Serena clone completed several days of immersion in an experimental cellular deceleration chamber, to slow the aging process. Her development had been stretched and pushed, and her weak biological body had endured incredible rigors.

The Tlulaxa had been anxious to prove his claims, but Erasmus reconsidered now. Thinking machines could wait for centuries, if necessary. Perhaps, if he decided to make another clone, he would allow that one to grow normally, since this experimental acceleration might have introduced flaws. The independent robot had extremely high expectations for his renewed interactions with Serena Butler. He did not want anything to get in the way.

As the gummy fluids drained and the female clone stood naked and dripping before him, Erasmus scrutinized her through several spectral regimes, using his full complement of optic threads. A long time ago, through his many surveillance systems, the robot had seen the original Serena naked many times; he had been present when she'd given birth to her frustrating infant, and he had personally performed the sterilization surgery on her so that the pregnancy problem could never occur again.

Now Rekur Van came forward, leering unpleasantly, to give her a physical examination, but Erasmus lifted the little Tlulaxa out of the way. He did not want Van to interfere with what should have been a special moment.

Still dripping from the tank, Serena didn't seem to care about her nudity, though the original would no doubt have been offended; just one of many personality variations that the robot noticed.

"Do I please you now?" Serena asked, blinking her lavender eyes. She stood seductively, as if trying to lure a potential mate. "I want you to like me."

An artificial scowl formed on Erasmus's flowmetal face, and his optic threads gleamed dangerously. Serena Butler had been haughty, independent, intelligent. Hating her captivity among the thinking machines, she had debated with Erasmus, searching for any chance to hurt him. She had *never* tried to please him.

"What did you do to her?" Erasmus turned to the Tlulaxa. "Why did she say that?"

Van smiled uncertainly. "Because of the acceleration, I had to guide her personality. I shaped it with standard female attitudes."

"Standard female attitudes?" Erasmus wondered if this unpleasant, isolated Tlulaxa man understood human women even less than *he* did. "There was nothing 'standard' about Serena Butler."

Van appeared increasingly uneasy, and he fell silent, deciding not to attempt further excuses. Erasmus remained more interested in the clone. This woman looked like Serena, in her soft, classically beautiful face and form, in her amber-brown hair, and in her unusual eyes.

But she wasn't the same. Only close enough to tickle his own memories of her, of the times they had spent together.

"Tell me your beliefs about politics, philosophy, and religion," the robot demanded. "Express your most impassioned feelings and opinions. Why do you think that even captive humans deserve to be treated with respect? Explain why you believe it is impossible for a thinking machine to achieve the equivalent of a human soul."

"Why do you wish to discuss such subjects?" She sounded almost petulant. "Tell me how you would like me to answer, so that I can please you."

As soon as the clone spoke, she shattered his fond remembrance of the real Serena. Though she looked exactly like Serena Butler, this simulacrum was very different in her internal makeup, the way she thought, the way she behaved. The cloned version had no social conscience, no spark, no glimmer of the personality that had become so familiar to him, and which had caused him so much interesting trouble. The real Serena's rebellious attitude had triggered an entire Jihad, while this poor substitute lacked any such potential.

Erasmus noted the difference in the glint of her eyes, in the turn of her mouth, in the way she threw her wet hair over her shoulder. He missed the fascinating woman he had known.

"Put your clothes on," Erasmus said. Looking on from one side, Rekur Van appeared alarmed, obviously sensing the robot's disappointment.

She slipped into the garments he had provided, accentuating her feminine curves. "Do you find me pleasing now?"

"No. Unfortunately, you are unacceptable."

With a blur of his flowmetal arm, Erasmus struck a swift, precise blow. He didn't want her to suffer, yet he did not want to look at this flawed clone ever again. With all his robotic strength, he drove the sharp edge of his shaped metal hand into the base of her neck, and decapitated her as easily as he might cut a flower in his greenhouse gardens. She made no sound as her head tumbled away and her body fell, spraying blood on his clean laboratory floor.

Such a disappointment.

On his left Rekur Van made a choking sound, as if he had forgotten how to breathe. The Tlulaxa man stumbled backward, but sentinel robots stood all around the laboratory chambers. The numerous tortured experimental subjects moaned and chattered in their cages, tanks, and tables.

Erasmus took a step toward the genetics researcher. Van held up his hands and his expression telegraphed what would occur next. As usual, he would try to worm his way out of any responsibility. "I did everything possible! Her DNA matches perfectly, and she is the same in every physical characteristic."

"She is not the same. You did not know the real Serena Butler."

"Yes! I met her. I took the tissue samples myself when she visited Bandalong!"

Erasmus made his flowmetal face a bland expressionless mirror. "You did not *know* her." This Tlulaxa's ability to perfectly recreate Serena Butler had been overstated, at best. As in the robot's own attempts to imitate the paintings of Van Gogh to the finest detail, the copy never approached the original's perfection.

"I have many more cells. This was just our first attempt, and we can try again. Next time, I'm sure we'll take care of the problems. That clone was different only because she never shared the real Serena's life experiences, never faced the same challenges. We can modify the virtual-reality teaching loops, make her spend more time immersed in sensory deprivation."

Erasmus shook his head. "She will never be what I want."

"Killing me would be a mistake, Erasmus! You can still learn much."

Staring at the Tlulaxa, the inquisitive robot noted how objectively unpleasant he was; apparently, all of his condemned breed were similar. Van had none of the noble attributes of character that could be found in so many people of other races. The little man might have some value after all, providing a new window on the dark side of human nature.

He was reminded of one of his thought-provoking signs. *Is it more human to be Good? Or Evil?*

The robot's flowmetal face formed into a broad smile.

"Why are you looking at me that way?" Van asked, nervously.

At a silent, transmitted signal from Erasmus, the sentinel robots came closer to surround the Tlulaxa man. Van had no place to run.

"Yes, I can learn from you, Rekur Van." He turned, his plush robe swirling, and signaled for the sentinel robots to seize the man. "In fact, I already have several very interesting experiments in mind …."

The Tlulaxa screamed.

✿ ✿ ✿

Fixing his gaze forward, Vorian Atreides sat stiffly on the bridge of the flagship. Over the past week, his assault force had been cruising across space. Soldiers and mercenaries continued their specialized drills. To the last man, they counted the days until reaching their next destination.

As the fleet entered Synchronized space, Vor mentally tallied all the weapons and firepower, all the soldiers and Ginaz mercenaries he would bring to bear against the thinking machines in the next great battle. He had not heard of the target planet before, but nevertheless Vor intended to conquer it and destroy the machine scourge.

Politics be damned. Out here is exactly where I belong.

For years after the death and defamation of Xavier, Vor had thrown himself into the struggle against Omnius. He fought one accursed machine enemy after another, striking in the sacred name of humanity.

Vor felt instilled with the holy determination of Serena, and of Xavier as well. Their strength allowed him to carry the Jihad forward. Always forward. He vowed anew to crush every thinking machine in his path. He would leave the next planet a blackened blister if there was no other way, despite the loss of unfortunate human slaves who served Omnius. By now, the Primero had learned to accept almost any cost in blood, just as long as it counted as a victory against the machines.

His two dearest friends had become martyrs in their own fashion. They had known what they were doing and had been willing to make great sacrifices, not only of their lives, but of their memories as well, allowing myths to replace truth, for the sake of the Jihad.

In a private message, Serena Butler had begged Vor and Xavier to understand the personal sacrifice she was making. Later, Xavier made his own sacrifice in order to stop the Grand Patriarch's predatory organ-farm scheme with the Tlulaxa, saving thousands of lives in the process. Xavier's decision to leave Iblis's name untarnished was unselfish and heroic; he knew full well how much harm would befall the Jihad if its Grand Patriarch was proven to be a fraud and a war profiteer.

Both Xavier and Serena had paid terrible, ultimate costs, with full knowledge of what they were doing. *I cannot dispute the decisions of my friends,* Vor thought, feeling a universe of sadness on his shoulders.

And he realized that his own burden must be to *let them do what they intended.* He had to resist the impulse to change what Xavier and Serena had done, and to let the untruths stand in order to achieve a long-term result. In accepting their fates and accomplishing what they had hoped, Serena and Xavier had left Vor to carry on in their behalf, and to bear an unseen banner of honor for all three of them.

Not an easy task, but that was my sacrifice.

"We are approaching the target planet, Primero," called his navigator.

On the flagship's screens, he saw the unremarkable planet— wispy clouds, blue oceans, brown and green land masses. And a bristling force of weirdly beautiful machine warships converging to form a defensive line. Even from a distance, the angular robotic battle vessels flickered with bursts of fire as they launched machine-guided projectiles in a hailstorm toward the League fleet.

"Engage our Holtzman shields." Vor rose from his chair and smiled confidently to the officers on the bridge with him. "Summon the Ginaz mercenaries into ground teams, ready to shuttle down as soon as we break the orbital defenses." He spoke automatically, confidently.

Decades ago, Serena had started this Jihad to avenge the murder of her baby. Xavier had fought beside Vor, crushing many machine foes. Now Vor, without his friends, intended to see this impossible war through to its end. It was the only way he could be sure the martyrs had made worthwhile sacrifices.

"Forward!" Vor raised his voice as the first robotic shells impacted against the Holtzman shields. "We have enemies to destroy!"

Red Plague

Introduction

Eighty years after the final defeat of the thinking machines, the human race began to build the Imperium under the Corrinos, who took their name from the victory at the Battle of Corrin. In the Schools of Dune trilogy—*Sisterhood of Dune, Mentats of Dune,* and *Navigators of Dune*—we told the saga of the formation of the seminal schools, the Bene Gesserit Sisterhood, the Mentat human computers, and the Spacing Guild and the Navigators.

The core of this trilogy is the war between faith and reason, fanaticism versus science. After centuries of the Jihad, and previous centuries of enslavement by computers and thinking machines, the Butlerian fanatics led by Manford Toronto want to destroy any hint of high technology, even where it is beneficial to humanity, while the rational demagogue Josef Venport wants to advance humanity by controlling and exploiting technology. Venport and Manford become mortal enemies, a clash of fundamentally opposed philosophies.

In this story, after the fledgling Imperium has been torn in half by civil war, the fanatics have to decide whether to accept help for a dying population, if it means admitting the benefits of science.

Red Plague

Even in his dreams, he could still hear the long-ago cheering and feel the energy and heartfelt dedication of the crowd. It roared around him, making his sleep restless. Young Manford Torondo could see the beatific face of Rayna Butler, his inspiration, his beloved mentor—whose vision had brought healing and faith to the human race after the bloody generations-long Jihad.

He could see Rayna's lips moving, but Manford could no longer remember the words she was speaking, because at that moment he had seen the bomb, had known it would explode. He rushed the stage, trying to save her, trying to throw himself upon the destructive device.

But it was too late.

The explosion was like a sun ripping open, right next to Rayna. He saw the shock wave, felt the flames, the energy that ripped bodies apart, destroyed the stage, sent fire and smoke and debris in all directions. Manford didn't feel his own pain, even though he had been close to the blast, much too close. He saw the mangled remnants of Rayna Butler, her clothing splashed red, her skin torn and lacerated. Frantic, he tried to run to her, tried to reach her, but for some reason he could barely move. He had nothing left but to crawl, and so he crawled.

It was only later that he realized he no longer had his legs. The blast had torn away the lower half of his body, leaving only gruesome shreds below his hips. But his own wounds were utterly unimportant. He had to get to Rayna, had to save her, to hold her somehow. Though his ruined body was only moments from catatonic shock, he used his bloody elbows to haul himself forward. He got to Rayna, touched her, looked into her eyes, and he imagined he saw the light still there, but fading. Finally, he summoned the energy to scream ....

He screamed now as firm hands shook him by the shoulders, and he woke in his narrow bed, his truncated body covered by a rough woolen blanket.

"Manford, you had that nightmare again," said Anari Idaho, his tall and muscular Swordmaster, his guardian, his most devoted companion. She loomed over him, her face filled with concern. "Rayna still haunts you, doesn't she?"

Manford swallowed in a dry throat and let her help him into a sitting position. "Rayna still blesses me with her memories. Even the most horrific vision of her is still *her*. Rayna was better than us all." He sighed. "Yet the burden falls to me to do the best I can to carry on her work. I must save the soul of humanity from its own temptation."

◊ ◊ ◊

"The people of Walgis are dying, Directeur, and they are crying out for help."

The black-garbed Mentat, Draigo Roget, issued his report in the offices of Josef Venport on the industrialist's capital world of Kolhar. The plight of that primitive planet sparked little sympathy in Venport's mind. He stroked his thick, cinnamon-colored mustache and frowned, sitting straight at his desk in the headquarters tower. He was the Directeur of Venport Holdings, a huge commercial empire that was now under siege and outlawed by the new Emperor Roderick Corrino. Venport was more concerned with his own dire situation than a few sick zealots.

"Let them cry," he said. "Let them plead." He allowed himself a small smile. "Let them reconsider their decision to follow the Butlerian nonsense and turn their backs on reason and civilization. One should expect plagues and diseases on a world that shuns even the most basic tenets of medicine."

Sighing, Venport sat back at his desk. His company was in turmoil, his commercial space fleet made technically illegal by Imperial decrees, yet still functioning because the Imperium needed their trade, needed their precious materials. They needed Josef Venport.

"The people of Walgis made their own decision when they chose to side with the barbarian half-Manford," he said. "I made my terms clear to them. Why should I help them now?"

The lean Mentat stood motionless, like a statue. His expression was blank. "Because one might wish to consider the bigger picture, Directeur. This is our chance to cause serious psychological damage to the Butlerian movement."

Draigo's gaze was intense and his thoughts well-ordered, as he'd been trained to do in the now-overthrown Mentat School on Lampadas. He stood by, waiting for his words to sink in. Venport knew that Draigo gave good and well-considered advice, even though he was reluctant to hear it.

The Directeur had spent many years building his multi-planet empire, developing mutant Navigators who could guide foldspace ships safely across the Imperium. Venport had drawn together the best technology that had survived Serena Butler's Jihad and now tried to rebuild weary humanity to a new golden age, while Manford's fanatics wanted a new dark age. Yes, the Jihad had overthrown the horrific thinking machines and freed all of humanity ... but freeing humanity did not mean reducing them to Stone-Age primitives. All high technology should not be discarded.

But the Butlerians believed exactly that. Led by Manford Torondo, the zealots wanted to reduce humanity to a primitive agrarian culture scattered across the galaxy. Josef Venport found himself entirely at odds with the legless freak.

Many planets had taken the Butlerian pledge, refusing the advances and benefits offered by Venport Holdings, and so he had imposed a retaliatory blockade on such worlds, refusing to deliver cargo or services until they renounced Manford's foolishness. He had hoped to make them see reason.

Walgis was one such world, and now they were in desperate straits. The red plague, a highly contagious and swiftly spreading disease, had appeared among the population. Thousands were already dead, tens of thousands infected and suffering, and the disease showed no sign of slowing.

"It seems to me that the plague is reducing the numbers of Butlerian fanatics," Venport said. "Tell me, Mentat, why is that not a good thing?"

"They're asking for help, Directeur, and providing such assistance would be a simple thing for us. Even Emperor Roderick could not criticize such an obvious humanitarian gesture. Perhaps it would soften his heart toward you."

"I don't care about the Emperor," Venport said.

"Yes, you do, sir, because your current status as an outlaw adversely affects your business dealings."

Venport frowned, but he could not deny the logic.

Draigo turned to the doorway, raised his hand in a signal, and a thin, small-statured man entered, wearing a loose white robe. The newcomer had long, steel-gray hair and a pointed beard at the tip of his chin. "Directeur, I wish to introduce you to Dr. Rohan Zim, who has come to us from the Suk Medical School on Parmentier. He urged me to help him make his case to you."

Intrigued by the visitor, Venport put his elbows on the desk, steepled his fingers, and looked at the Suk-trained doctor. "Why can't he make his own case?"

Zim hurried forward. "I will, Directeur Venport." From a pocket, he produced a data crystal, which he inserted into the player embedded in Venport's desk. Like mist rising on a cool morning, images appeared in the air, holographic recordings that showed miserable people lying in endless lines of rickety beds. The victims writhed and moaned, their faces covered in perspiration, their skin tones grayish, their faces blotched with scarlet eruptions. "As you can see, Directeur, the red plague is terrible. It will continue to spread, but we can do something about it."

"You mean impose a quarantine?" Venport asked. "We don't want any infected people to get out and spread the disease to other populated worlds, especially those that are highly civilized."

Draigo said, "Manford Torondo's Butlerian ships are already in orbit, enforcing their own blockade. The people of Walgis have little enough capability for space travel as it is. They are being kept confined without any interference from us."

The Suk doctor interjected, "And even if it were to spread, the disease is easily treatable with modern medicine. That is why I am here, Directeur. We have readily available vaccines. On Parmentier, the Suk Medical School has been manufacturing the necessary drugs to cure the red plague—provided we can deliver them to the sick. And for that we need the assistance of the Ven-Hold Spacing Fleet."

Venport frowned. "Again, I must ask, why does it serve my purposes to save barbarians who want to destroy me?"

Rohan Zim gave the Directeur a dark look. "At the Suk Medical School, we all swear an oath to tend the sick and dying, to treat those who need our medical expertise."

Venport made a dismissive gesture. "You speak to me of altruism? Can you not make a better argument?"

The Mentat took a step closer, meeting Venport's gaze even as the holo-images of the miserable plague victims continued to play in the air above the desk. "It would be a good business decision, I believe. The Suk Medical School is already offering the vaccines and treatments, so long as we provide transport. It would cost you little, yet we could make it apparent that you—Directeur Josef Venport—are the savior of this world. It will prove to all, not just to Emperor Roderick, that you are a good man who is willing to take the high road. After you save Walgis, you might even win over the people there, make them reconsider their decision to side with the Butlerians." The Mentat shrugged. "It's possible."

Venport mulled over the idea, saw the implications. He smiled. "Ah, and it would be a victory over the half-Manford. It would show me to be superior." Then he gave a brisk nod. "Very well, Dr. Zim. Gather your vaccines and treatments, and I'll provide one of our smaller ships to transport you to Walgis. Save those people in my name, whether or not they deserve it."

✧ ✧ ✧

Anari Idaho lit a lamp, which shed a warm, golden glow throughout Manford's private quarters in his small cottage on Lampadas. "The people love you just as you loved Rayna," she said to him. "You are the voice of the Butlerians. You are the soul of humanity, the only thing that keeps us from slipping back into the clutches of the evil thinking machines."

"And the demon Venport with his cursed technology," Manford said.

Anari gave a brusque nod. "I consider them one and the same, and that is why this news is disturbing. We have more reports from Walgis, where the red plague continues to spread."

Manford lowered his head solemnly. "Do we know how many are dead?"

"Tens of thousands. Yet our blockade and quarantine holds. They will not escape and infect others, but no one has ventured to the surface to tend them directly."

He gave another nod. "As I ordered."

"Our warships enforce the cordon, and it is holding. But the people …" She drew a breath and shook her head. "They are desperate, Manford. They're begging you for help."

"I am very moved by this tragedy," he said. "The people of Walgis are my most devoted followers. They were among the first to take the Butlerian pledge, shunning all technology and cutting themselves off from temptations. They have remained strong. They would suffer anything for me—you know that. I wish I could repay their loyalty somehow."

Anari lifted him up and helped him dress, even though his entire body ended below his hips. When he needed to travel, the Swordmaster would place him in a special harness on her back so she could carry him anywhere.

The answer was obvious, and he didn't hesitate. "I've decided what to do," he said. "Anari, you will accompany me to Walgis. I intend to join the quarantine fleet in orbit there and pray for the people who are suffering. I can watch over them and show them my love."

Anari nodded. "I like that idea. You can speak with them, give them comfort. You can bless them, even from orbit."

☼ ☼ ☼

The VenHold spacefolder, guided by one of the rare and mysterious Navigators, was the swiftest and most reliable means of transportation in the known universe. Even so, Dr. Rohan Zim found the delay agonizing as he waited for the ship to arrive at Walgis.

Ever since hearing about the deadly plague, he had tirelessly rallied the doctors at the new medical facilities on Parmentier. He wanted to save those people, even if they were Butlerians. A mob of the anti-technology fanatics had burned down the long-standing Suk Medical School on Salusa Secundus, and they had demonstrated against medical technology, even against basic surgical advances. The zealots considered sophisticated new prosthetics and artificial organs to be abhorrent. They railed against scientific progress that would have increased food production and saved countless lives.

Dr. Rohan Zim found very little to like about the backward Butlerians. But they were still *people*, and he had taken a solemn vow when he became a Suk doctor.

Upon receiving approval from Directeur Venport, Zim rushed back to Parmentier, where his people had been working nonstop to manufacture the vital vaccines and treatments for those afflicted. Despite its virulence, the red plague was an old disease, well recognized and mostly eradicated across human-settled planets. The cure existed; it just needed to be delivered to the sick.

The people on Walgis had to agree to the treatment, even if it had a strong basis in technology. Zim had no doubts, though: There was nothing like watching one's family moan and die in feverish misery to make a person reassess esoteric beliefs.

Dr. Zim and his Suk colleagues had created and packaged one hundred thousand doses of the cure. They would need help distributing and administering the vaccines, but his volunteers would teach others, who would in turn teach even more, and perhaps the red plague would be caught and stopped. Once those hundred thousand doses were delivered, the recovered victims would provide the antibodies to cure the rest. Zim wished his team had been able to begin a week sooner.

Now he joined the other doctors on the observation deck during the final foldspace jump to Walgis. When the Holtzman engines activated, there was only a brief distortion as space folded around the small vessel. The Navigator, in his murky tank of swirling gas, chose a path and guided the ship, and then emerged as ripples in the fabric of the universe smoothed out again, returning them to normal space just outside of Walgis.

One of the doctors pointed out the observation window at a bright dot that grew progressively larger as the spacefolder accelerated toward its destination. As the planet became a discernible disc, they could see bright lights, flickering shapes of large ships in orbit—battleships.

"Those will be the Butlerian vessels," Zim said. "A quarantine cordon to keep the infected from escaping. In that matter, at least, we can thank Manford Torondo."

He looked to the wall as his fellow doctors gathered at the observation window. He raised his voice to the VenHold crew, who were listening on the wall pickup. "Open a communication channel, please. I wish to address the planet Walgis as well as the quarantine ships. They will want to hear our good news."

Within moments the comm officer acknowledged that the channel was open, and Dr. Zim cleared his throat, straightened his white robes, brushed his beard flat, and looked at the image pickup on the wall.

"People of Walgis, we are doctors from the Suk Medical laboratories on Parmentier. We respect all life, without regard to political or religious beliefs. We know of your plight and are pleased to offer our assistance and expertise." He drew a breath and acknowledged their benefactor. "With the benevolence of Directeur Josef Venport, we have come here to help. Your suffering is nearly ended, and we will care for you and save as many as we possibly can." He smiled. "We have brought vaccines!"

✧ ✧ ✧

Aboard the quarantine fleet, Manford had been praying. He knew that all the people on the planet below were in his care—not just their fever-wracked and weak physical bodies, but their souls as well, for him to guide and advise. He helped them not to be weak when temptations were strong.

For three days now, ever since arriving to join the battleship cordon with the diligent Anari Idaho, Manford had addressed the entire planet. He spoke to the grieving and suffering people. He blessed them, knowing they took comfort in his compassionate words. With a gesture and a prayer, Manford Torondo, heir to the dreams of Rayna Butler, could bring hope and clarity, not just to those below who were doomed by the red plague, but to all of his followers, who would similarly draw strength from his heroic presence here at Walgis. Every Butlerian must know how Manford's heart ached when even one of his followers was harmed.

On the bridge of one of the Butlerian quarantine ships, Manford rode comfortably in the harness on Anari's shoulders. She had placed him there so that he could ride tall, his legless torso fitting neatly into the leather embrace. He was the commander, the great leader and visionary. He'd been staring down at the deceptively peaceful appearance of the planet below. Walgis, a staunchly loyal Butlerian world, had once been ravaged by thinking machines during the Jihad. The people had been crushed and tormented, but through adversity came strength. Manford was proud of them.

He'd been thinking about the explosion at Rayna's last rally, how he had lost the lower half of his body and yet emerged stronger than ever before with a sharper focus, and a greater determination—"Half a man, twice the leader." Those who survived down there would be even more fiercely loyal than the population had been before ....

And then the VenHold ship arrived over Walgis, a small vessel broadcasting a message of supposed hope and deceptive miracles. Manford felt his muscles tense as he reached down to hold onto Anari's shoulders, drawing strength from her. She felt as solid as an old tree.

"We have brought vaccines," said the Suk doctor aboard the approaching vessel.

His jaw ached as he gritted his teeth. Manford called all of his quarantine ships to high alert. Rather than turning their weapons toward the planet below to prevent escapees, now they focused their firepower outward, their crews ready to face this oncoming threat.

Manford broadcast to the population below, not bothering to respond directly to the VenHold ship. "You are strong enough without medicine. Our beloved Rayna Butler endured the most horrific plagues spread by the thinking machines; diseases far worse than the red plague. Her heart and soul were strong, and she recovered. Rayna recovered because *God* wanted her to recover, knowing she had greater work to do. God will make you recover as well."

He cut off the communication and looked at Anari, who gazed up at him with complete acceptance and reverence. All around the bridge of his flagship, he saw similar expressions, giving him assurance that every vessel in the quarantine cordon would react the same.

"We must protect them from the sinister influence," Manford said. "We have to safeguard my people from the insidious promises of the demon Venport, and from their own weaknesses."

Steeling himself, he sent another transmission. "To all the afflicted people of Walgis, rejoice! You are saved."

Then he gave the order for all of his battleships around the planet to target the incoming medical ship. He felt no hesitation, merely relief when he issued his instruction. "Open fire."

And his crews obeyed.

✿ ✿ ✿

Out on the Kolhar landing field, Josef Venport gazed at his numerous ships, a fleet of spacefolder transports and large cargo shuttles that would travel to orbit to dock with even larger carriers. These well-armed ships were an enhancement to his own defenses, in case Emperor Roderick ever got up the nerve to attack here.

Fueling tankers filled the reservoirs of the large ships. With a whistling roar, one of the cargo shuttles heaved itself from the launching platform and thundered up into the sky. On the field, heavy machinery moved about, giving him a satisfied feeling. His VenHold fleet kept delivering much-needed—and now higher-priced—cargo to any planets in the Imperium that could afford the payments. It almost seemed like business as usual.

Except the entire Imperium had turned on its head.

"It defies reason! This is more insane than Manford has been before." As he walked along, he clenched his fists and the black-garbed Draigo kept pace with gliding steps. "He destroyed our vessel, wiped out its cargo of vaccines, and left his own followers to rot from the pandemic. *And they cheered him as he did it!*"

Draigo gave a small nod. "In my Mentat projections, sir, I recognized a very small possibility that the Butlerians might react this way. I apologize for not giving it sufficient credence."

"No one could have predicted such a heinous response, Draigo," Venport said. "Even now that you've delivered your report, I still can't believe it. Manford has doomed his people to die from a disease that is easily cured just because he doesn't want the help to come from me. He's a madman and a mass murderer."

Venport felt disgusted as well as angry. He didn't really care about the dying barbarians on Walgis. As far as he was concerned, they could all suffer horribly from the red plague. And truth be told, he lost only one small ship, easily replaced, and a few Suk doctors who weren't even his employees. As a business loss, Venport could easily overcome it. But it was so damned outrageous! He was having a very hard time believing the half-Manford's immoral act.

Draigo Roget shook his head. "It defies logic. If I am to make more accurate projections about our opponent, I shall have to learn to think more irrationally."

Venport stopped to watch a delivery vehicle bearing a sealed container of spice gas, pumping it into one of the ships to fill a Navigator's sealed tank. He considered all the battles he had fought, his struggles to save humanity and rebuild civilization, to overcome the scars the thinking machines had left … as well as his struggles against the inept and foolhardy Emperor Salvador. For the good of all humankind, Venport had replaced Salvador with his brother Roderick, a man he believed to be more rational—although Roderick was now more interested in revenge than in strengthening his Imperium.

"Sometimes I despair for humanity, and wonder why I continue this desperate and ruthless fight," Venport said with a dismayed sigh. "Even after the defeat of the thinking machines and my constant struggles to help our race recover, the Butlerian fanatics remain.

I fear they are our worst enemy. They will destroy our future as surely as any army of thinking machines ever could. The barbarians must be destroyed. No matter what weapons we must use or what sacrifices we must make, we have to crush Manford Torondo and his followers at all costs."

"I agree, Directeur," said Draigo.

Venport felt confident, though not arrogant. The Butlerian movement was comprised of primitives, rabid barbarians, while VenHold had the most sophisticated technology in the Imperium. "They are no match for us," he said.

Beside him, Draigo did not respond, but his brow furrowed as he reviewed the facts. Venport strode ahead, assessing his ships and other resources.

When the Mentat responded, he spoke so quietly that Venport almost didn't hear his words. "And yet, I fear they will win."

The Dune Period

Wedding Silk

Introduction

Part of our novel *Paul of Dune* details the early years of Paul Atreides and his training under Duncan Idaho and two other Swordmasters, Rivvy Dinari and Whitmore Bludd.

Even though Duke Leto loves his concubine Jessica, Paul's mother, he has to forge a marriage alliance with the daughter of Archduke Armand Ecaz in order to protect House Atreides from the complex political forces arrayed against them. To finalize the betrothal, Duke Leto brings Paul and Jessica, along with Duncan Idaho, to the Archduke's court on the jungled planet of Ecaz.

We originally wrote this story as part of *Paul of Dune*, but during the final edits of the manuscript we decided the events were not essential to the main plot, and so we edited it from the final published version of the novel.

Wedding Silk

Paul watched his mother in the withdrawing room of the Ecaz palace. Jessica seemed stoic and unruffled, not at all troubled about being left alone, and showing no sign that the situation bothered her. She accepted the reason for which she, the Duke, and their son had come to this rich and verdant planet. She treated Duke Leto's upcoming wedding as if it were merely a commercial transaction, like shipping salted fish or investing in pharmaceutical commodities.

Jessica's ability to play a role was masterful, her demeanor perfect. To anyone else, her mask was a flawless disguise, but Paul noticed subtle indicators, hidden reactions, the tiniest flutter of an eyelid. His mother had taught him well—she didn't fool him for a moment.

The Lady Jessica was Duke Leto's concubine and companion, but not a wife. "I have always known and accepted this, Paul. I'm not a giddy schoolgirl who reads too many romantic poems." She wanted him to believe her aloof expression. "Marriage is a business alliance, a political weapon to be used for the advancement of House Atreides in the Landsraad. Love is ... its own thing." Her reassuring smile would have convinced anyone else. "Our hearts may confuse the two, but our minds must not. And a *human* makes life choices with the mind, not based on the chemical tug-of-war of emotions."

Paul's sympathy went out to his mother, and he stayed with her in this lonely room, though he longed to explore the crowded, whispering jungles of Ecaz, which were so unlike even the tropical areas of Caladan. Through the palace's open windows the scent of pollens wafted in the air, along with the lush humidity wafting from the riot of vegetation. He put aside the temptations of this exotic place.

As the Atreides heir, he would have to join the wedding party and participate in the ceremony. Knowing that his mother wanted him to understand, and determined to play his role as convincingly as she did, Paul said, "Lady Ilesa Ecaz seems an acceptable match for my father. Joining our families will benefit House Atreides greatly."

Paul's mother could see through him, as well, and she shooed him out of her chamber. "You are still the Duke's firstborn son, Paul. Learn and experience everything you can—it will make you a more balanced leader. Speak with Duncan. He and the Archduke's Swordmasters can show you Ecaz. This is an opportunity for you. Take advantage of it."

Paul hesitated at the doorway. Outside, he heard a bird call, an eerie melodic keening, like an avian siren song; he wondered what it was. "You'll be all right?"

Jessica busied herself with a sheaf of accounting records, which had seemed unimportant only moments before. "Go. I have plenty to keep me occupied."

✧ ✧ ✧

Duncan Idaho regarded the two Swordmasters: the foppish Whitmore Bludd and the enormously fat but agile Rivvy Dinari. "It is Duke Leto's wish that Paul see more of this planet than the Archduke's residence."

Dressed in elegant clothes, Bludd raised his eyebrows at the suggestion. "If this is the boy's first time on Ecaz, we must take him out to the fogtree forests. It's an experience he'll never forget."

Though Paul stood with the three men, they discussed him as if he didn't exist. He wanted to make them pay attention. "It is my wish as well. I've read about Ecazi fogtrees in filmbooks, and I found the images very interesting."

"Pah!" Dinari chuckled. "Images are nothing. You must see the fogtrees with your own eyes. I'll go requisition an ornithopter, so we can fly out immediately. There's a whole planet to see, and we'd better get started."

Duncan was somewhat cautious. "This is the Duke's son. We will have to guarantee his safety."

Bludd rolled his eyes in disbelief. "Are we not three Swordmasters from Ginaz?"

✧ ✧ ✧

The ornithopter fluttered away from the Archduke's ethereal palace, rising into the clouds and heading west over forested hills that rapidly gave way to steep mountains and sheltered valleys. Overarching trees formed a thick canopy that enclosed a shadowy and mysterious underworld. Paul leaned close to the 'thopter's curved windowplaz, drinking in the amazing sight, although he tried not to seem too overawed; he doubted he fooled the three Swordmasters.

Kite-sized butterflies drifted languidly along beside the aircraft. As the 'thopter dipped toward a broad artificial platform built into the upthrust crown of a tree, a clump of the supposed leaves took flight, revealing themselves to be green-camouflaged moths. Paul let out a laugh, while Bludd, at the piloting controls, merely complained and dodged around the dispersing insects.

The ornithopter settled down in a vacant spot on the landing platform. Several vehicles were parked there in the sunlight—exploration or harvesting crews working in the underforest—but Paul saw no one else around. He climbed out of the 'thopter and went to the edge of the platform, where thin metal cables extended from the platform's edge like the spokes of a wheel, plunging through the canopy to connect with lower platforms that were mounted to the trunks of other trees.

Next to Paul, Bludd peered down to where dense leaves swallowed the cables. He pointed. "Pharmaceutical prospectors have a cargo lifter at the base of this main tree, which they use to load their harvest and haul it up from the underbrush. But we'll take a faster route down to the forest floor."

97

The Swordmasters rummaged through a strongbox near the landed 'thopter and withdrew harnesses and hooks. Bludd took great care to demonstrate the techniques, showing both Duncan and Paul how to fit the harness properly about their bodies. Duncan approved Paul's equipment before he checked his own, satisfying himself that the young man had made no mistakes.

As he strapped on his equipment, Rivvy Dinari looked like a whale wrestling with a fishing net. Finished, Dinari walked to the edge of the platform and clipped his harness to a trolley mechanism on the cable. "Watch me." Paul could hear the platform planks groan under the big man's weight as he leaned back into his sturdy harness. "These ziplines are fast, but perfectly safe."

"We had to specially reinforce that cable to carry Dinari's weight," Bludd quipped.

"My weight allows me to achieve greater velocity. It's an advantage."

"Only if the tree itself doesn't break," Bludd said.

With a snort, Dinari lifted his feet, swung out over the gulf, and released himself. He streaked down the zipline and plunged into the leafy depths of the canopy, swallowed up by a tunnel carved through the foliage.

"It's quite simple, actually." Bludd hooked his own gear onto the line and glanced over his shoulder at Duncan. "The hard part is stopping yourself in time. If you strike a tree trunk, you'll most assuredly stop, but that's not the recommended technique." In a moment, he whisked away down the zipline.

Without waiting for Duncan's approval, Paul said, "I'm next." He followed the lead of the other two and found himself soaring along the descending cable, his legs suspended. As he raced through the thick leaves, picking up speed, the wind whistled past; above his head, the trolley sang on the cable.

Ahead, the terminal platform came up fast, but two Swordmasters waited for him with outstretched arms. Dinari caught Paul like an enormous mattress, stopping him, and Bludd swung him onto the platform and disengaged the harness hook in a swift motion, moving him off of the cable. Paul laughed breathlessly with exhilaration. Duncan arrived a few moments later.

Using three successive ziplines, they worked their way down-ward to the lush and entirely foreign underworld on the forest floor.

❖ ❖ ❖

In the undergrowth at the base of the fogtrees, a constant rustle moved through the rotted soil and tangle of fallen branches. The dense brush was alive with hidden creatures, buzzing insects, spiky fungi, and golden ferns that unfurled and furled.

Bludd tagged the coordinates of the massive tree that supported the landing platform high above, and kept a small locator device at his hip. Duncan scouted the green shadows, narrowing his eyes. "Turn on your body shield for protection, Paul."

The boy did as he was told, and Duncan followed suit. The other two Swordmasters nodded at the precaution. Dinari reached around his belt and activated the humming field that extended across his girth. "Things can get unpredictable down here."

"At least it'll hinder these incessant insects." Bludd swatted at the air for good measure, though he didn't seem to be targeting any particular bug. "If we encounter any danger, three of us can hide in a protective little cranny and use Rivvy, here, as a blockade."

The fat Swordmaster, taking no offense at the constant ribbing, responded in kind. "I am honored to serve in any capacity, even if it's only to prevent your fine garments from getting soiled—unless, of course, you happen to soil yourself. In that event, I'm afraid I can't help you."

Bludd took the lead, and they trotted along, exploring interest-ing foliage. Cocking his head to hear a crunching rustle, Dinari lifted fallen sheets of bark to show Paul a nest of scuttling emerald beetles that were the size of his hand. Puffball mushrooms exploded nearby, and Bludd quickly knocked his companions in the other direction. "Don't inhale! Those are hallucinogenic spores."

Paul held his breath until they were at a safe distance.

Ahead of them, he heard a buzzing rustle of sound that swelled like a roaring fire, and Duncan glanced around warily. "What is that?"

"That is exactly what we wanted to hear," Bludd said. "Since your Duke announced his upcoming wedding to Lady Ilesa, I thought you and the young lad would like to obtain a betrothal present un-like anything else the Duke is bound to receive."

"Bludd has a fine eye for gifts," Dinari said. "I think he would prefer shopping to fighting."

Leading their guests, the two Swordmasters parted the fronds of two-meter-high ferns to reveal a clearing. The swell of sound—like an armful of crackling paper—grew louder, and Paul saw that it came from a tangled mass of branches, leaves, and *silvery webs*. The silky webs enclosed twigs and thick boughs in a mummy-wrapped cocoon that filled the glade.

"Ever see anything like that on Caladan, boy?" Dinari asked.

Duncan put an arm out to stop Paul when he tried to press forward for a better view. "No, sir," Paul answered in a quiet voice.

"Don't worry—they're still enclosed," Bludd announced. "We should be safe. The caterpillars won't range about until the food inside the tent is all gone—another few weeks yet."

They all stepped forward in wonder. Thick ropes of silk hung, glued to fallen trees and rocks, stretching out as awnings to hold the translucent gossamer sheets.

"We've been watching this nest for some time, and it's about as ready as it could be," the foppish Swordmaster continued. "The silk is truly remarkable."

"*You've* been watching it." Dinari laughed. "I couldn't give a fig for silk."

"Because you have no taste in clothing." Bludd turned to Paul and Duncan, ignoring the fat Swordmaster. "This webbing has the perfect sheen and a soft, comfortable hand. Lady Ilesa could want nothing better for wedding silk."

Hearing this, Paul wished instead that he could give it to his mother, but she would turn it down. Jessica played her role, and the Bene Gesserit had taught her to control every aspect of her heart and mind. And Paul had his role to play as well. "Yes, it would make a fine gift for my father's new wife. Thank you for thinking of it for me."

Bludd drew his dagger and motioned for Duncan and Paul to follow him, while Dinari trudged into the clearing under the tentlike structure. Within the folds of spun fabric, Paul could see shadowy cylindrical forms. The shadows of the ominous vermiform creatures shifted behind the gauze, raising a chill in him. They loomed up, then faded from view, seen and unseen.

Paul had dreamed of huge worms several times, creatures much larger than these—behemoths that lived beneath a shifting surface … majestic and also mysterious. He remembered being terrified, yet awestruck, waking without understanding. He had described the dreams to his mother, but she had no explanation for what the images might mean. The metaphors delivered by his subconscious could be interpreted many ways; the serpentine leviathans in his dreams might be a symbol of strength, or a shapeless threat.

These occasional vivid dreams confused Paul. Were they premonitions or merely nightmares? Either way, he did not understand them.

"Falcon-moths are responsible for the nests, boy," Dinari explained. "Isn't your Atreides house crest a falcon?"

"No, it's a hawk." Paul said it with enough conviction to imply a vast metaphorical distinction between the two raptors, though he would have been hard-pressed to explain it.

The fat Swordmaster didn't seem to care about the subtleties. "When the caterpillars hatch, they eat their egg casings and devour all the nearby foliage as they spin a larger and larger tent complex. Then they eat the branches and the heartwood, and when the supporting trees are dead, the caterpillars eat one another. Only the strongest ones tear their way out of the tent-cocoon. By then, they are near starving, and they go on a rampage through the underbrush. You can find large dead areas and clearings where the worms have hatched."

"That's why you have to be careful." Bludd slashed one of the anchor strands with the tip of his dagger. "Don't break through the main containment wall when harvesting the silk."

"*We* won't," Duncan said pointedly.

With great care, Bludd peeled away the flat filmy sheet of tent-silk and wrapped it like a large bolt of cloth on his arm. Paul was reminded of a vendor in the Caladan market who spun sweet sugar into clouds of candy on a stick.

With his body shield still on, Paul took up his dagger and found another anchor point, imitating Bludd's technique. The raw tent-silk had a slick, airy feel. From the nest came the sounds of squirming, twitching. He guessed there must be more than a thousand large caterpillars crowded together, all famished by now.

Bludd finished wrapping up a large roll of the silk, set it aside, and began to extract more. Dinari, with a put-upon air, also began to cut some of the silk free. While Paul worked with the other two men to gather his unique wedding gift, Duncan kept watch for danger in the thriving underbrush.

Duncan suddenly ducked, craned his neck as a shadow flitted through the leaves overhead. "Careful!" He held up his sword.

With a fluttering buzz, two large shapes streaked just above them, circled the matted silky mess, then darted back up above the canopy. Paul jerked his head upward, following them.

"Those were falcon-moths," Dinari said. "Sometimes they guard their nests."

"We are being very careful," Bludd said in a whisper, apparently talking to himself. "Gentle … gentle …"

With a twang, he severed another anchor-cord, but this one snapped and recoiled from the tension. As Bludd scrambled out of the way, numerous layers of interlinked fabric started to unravel and split apart. "*That* wasn't supposed to happen."

"Duncan!" Paul yelled. "Trouble!"

And then, as the sheet of fabric tore open, widening the rift, caterpillars roiled out of the nest like armloads of giant maggots. The segmented creatures were a sickly, pale green, their bodies adorned with yellow spots. The shortest worms were as long as his arm; others were as thick as his thigh and nearly a meter and a half in length.

The caterpillar heads were like smooth eyeless helmets sporting a set of clacking mandibles made for chewing wood. From each thorax sprouted six pointed legs that opened and closed, reaching for something to grasp. Paul saw that many tentworms were scarred and scratched from doing combat in the confines of the tent; some worms oozed gelatinous green ichor from tears in their skin. Now freed, the caterpillars lunged toward anything that moved—including Paul and the three Swordmasters.

Bludd sheathed his cutting knife and instead whipped out his thin rapier. With a flourish, he lunged forward, skewering a caterpillar and flinging it aside so he could stab the next.

"Stay out of this, Paul," Duncan yelled. He sliced open the side of a worm with the tip of the Old Duke's sword. "Get out of the clearing—I don't want you hurt."

"You trained me yourself." Paul brandished his knife. "There are plenty of worms for all of us to kill."

"Lad, you've got that right!" Dinari began slashing and chopping, butchering a dozen of the squirming bugs in only a few seconds as they tumbled toward the four intruders.

Bludd scowled at a splurt of ichor across his chest. "Bloody Hell, Rivvy! You're a Swordmaster of Ginaz—use a bit of finesse! People will think you grew up in a slaughterhouse."

Two caterpillars turned their spinnerets toward the wiry Swordmaster and sprayed fresh webbing on his tunic and trousers. While Bludd clawed the sticky strands away, Dinari gave him a wry look. "You're right, Bludd—the silk does look good on you."

When one of the tentworms reared up in front of Paul, he stabbed the smooth head with his dagger, but the knife glanced off the chitin. Turning the dagger, he thrust again, this time jamming the point between the worm's mandibles, then twisting. He kicked the heavy carcass aside.

The other men did not pause in their mayhem. Bludd taunted from the side, "That's fifteen for me so far, Rivvy. What's your count?"

"Pah. I don't have time to count!

A squirt of slime splashed onto Bludd's face and across his ruffled tunic. Scowling, he skewered the offending worm twice for good measure. Worms still spilled from the tent, but many more carcasses lay inside, their flaccid empty bodies gnawed by their stronger brothers.

Soon dead caterpillars lay everywhere. Their squirming and squeaking sounds filled the glade, along with the slash-and-squish of hard fighting. Paul killed three more. Fighting at Duncan's side, he waited for a group of four to lunge at them, then together they slashed and cut.

"I was hoping for the chance to train you under practical conditions, Master Paul," Duncan said.

Paul grinned. "And how am I doing so far?"

From the corner of his eye, a flash of motion alerted him. He spun and ducked simultaneously, but not fast enough. A falcon-moth came at him like a dive-bomber, its long narrow wings like an ornithopter's, its head torpedo-shaped. The moth slammed into Paul, moving too fast to pass through the shimmering body shield. The impact sent the moth reeling, and a dusty cloud of dislodged scales from its wings blew everywhere.

The falcon-moth's antennae waved like feathers, each as wide as Paul's outstretched hand. Its wings drummed against the shield as it tried to orient itself and dive in again, but Duncan slashed its abdomen. Yellowish guts spilled out.

As the dying moth wheeled away, then came back, Paul's dagger caught the antennae. The creature flew away drunkenly and one wing caught in the loose fabric of the cocoon tent. After struggling like a fly in a spiderweb, the gutted moth crashed to the ground amid the dead caterpillars.

"Oho, a trophy for Duncan Idaho and his young companion!" Dinari bellowed. "Even I've never managed to kill a falcon-moth on the wing."

"Dirty things," Bludd spat.

Catching their breath, the Swordmasters strode about like scavengers in the aftermath on a battlefield, stabbing the few remaining worms and then wiping the slime from their blades.

"You did well, Paul," Duncan said, wiping ichor from his face.

"Now there's a battle to remember," Dinari added.

Bludd said in a singsong voice, "Young Paul Atreides, Conqueror of Caterpillars and Slayer of Squirmers! You have earned this wedding silk for your father's bride."

The boy walked over to the still-twitching, somehow sad form of the huge falcon-moth. "It was only trying to protect its nest. The silk didn't mean that much to me."

A shadowy, uneasy feeling came over him. A falcon and a hawk … how much difference was there? At the thought of what this moth had done, he felt a shudder of realization: Duke Leto would have done a similar thing, throwing himself into certain destruction if it was his only chance to save his family.

His family, Jessica and Paul … and now Ilesa Ecaz. And whatever children they might have. And how many others?

"On the bright side, we don't have to be careful any longer," Bludd said cheerfully. "We can retrieve all the tent-silk for ourselves. I've never had such an extravagant haul."

"It's going to be a very large wedding for Duke Leto." Duncan smiled at Paul, sure his young ward must be excited about the upcoming celebration.

But Paul could only see all the strands of silk, the tangled webs, and the dead falcon-moth that lay among its slaughtered young.

A Whisper of Caladan Seas

Introduction

We have written a million and a half words in the Dune universe, fourteen books—plus this one—but this story is connected to none of them. "A Whisper of Caladan Seas" is actually a side tale within the original novel *Dune*, taking place concurrent with the Harkonnen attack on the Atreides stronghold of Arrakeen.

A Whisper of Caladan Seas

Arrakis, in the year 10,191 of the Imperial calendar. Arrakis … forever known as Dune ….

The cave in the massive Shield Wall was dark and dry, sealed by an avalanche. The air tasted like rock dust. The surviving Atreides soldiers huddled in blackness to conserve energy, letting their glowglobe power packs recycle.

Outside, the Harkonnen shelling hammered against the bolthole where they had fled for safety. Artillery? What a surprise to be attacked by such seemingly obsolete technology … and yet, it was effective. *Damned effective.*

In pockets of silence that lasted only seconds, the young recruit Elto Vitt lay in pain listening to the wheezing of wounded, terrified men. The stale, oppressive air pressed heavy on him, increasing the broken-glass agony in his lungs. He tasted blood in his mouth, an unwelcome moisture in the absolute dryness.

His uncle, Sergeant Hoh Vitt, had not honestly told him how severe his injuries were, emphasizing Elto's "youthful resilience and stamina." Elto suspected he must be dying, and he wasn't alone in that predicament. These last soldiers were all dying, if not from their injuries, then from hunger or thirst.

Thirst.

A man's voice cut the darkness, a gunner named Deegan. "I wonder if Duke Leto got away. I hope he's safe."

A reassuring grunt. "Thufir Hawat would slit his own throat before he'd let the Baron touch our Duke, or young Paul." It was the signalman Scovich, fiddling with the flexible hip cages that held two captive distrans bats, creatures whose nervous systems could carry message imprints.

"Bloody Harkonnens!" Then Deegan's sigh became a sob. "I wish we were back home on Caladan."

Supply Sergeant Vitt was no more than a disembodied voice in the darkness, comfortingly close to his injured young nephew. "Do *you* hear a whisper of Caladan seas, Elto? Do you hear the waves, the tides?"

The boy concentrated hard. Indeed, the relentless artillery shelling sounded like the booming of breakers against the glistening black rocks below the cliff-perch of Castle Caladan.

"Maybe," he said. But he didn't, not really. The similarity was only slight, and his uncle, a Master Jongleur … a storyteller extraordinaire … wasn't up to his capabilities, though here he couldn't have asked for a more attentive audience. Instead the sergeant seemed stunned by events, and uncharacteristically quiet, not his usual gregarious self.

Elto remembered running barefoot along the beaches on Caladan, the Atreides home planet far, far from this barren repository of dunes, sandworms, and precious spice. As a child, he had tiptoed in the foamy residue of waves, avoiding the tiny pincers of crabfish so numerous that he could net enough for a fine meal in only a few minutes.

Those memories were much more vivid than what had actually happened ….

✿ ✿ ✿

The alarms had rung in the middle of the night, ironically during the first deep sleep Elto Vitt had managed in the Atreides barracks at Arrakeen. Only a month earlier, he and other recruits had been assigned to this desolate planet, saying their farewells to lush

Caladan. Duke Leto Atreides had received the governorship of Arrakis, the only known source of the precious spice melange, as a boon from the Padishah Emperor Shaddam IV.

To many of the loyal Atreides soldiers, it had seemed a great financial coup—they had known nothing of politics … or of danger. Apparently Duke Leto had not been aware of the peril here either, because he'd brought along his concubine Lady Jessica and their fifteen-year-old son, Paul.

When the warning bells shrieked, Elto snapped awake and rolled from his bunk bed. His uncle Hoh Vitt, already in full sergeant's regalia, shouted for everyone to hurry, *hurry!* The Atreides house guard grabbed their uniforms, kits, and weapons. Elto recalled allowing himself a groan, annoyed at another apparent drill … and yet hoping it was only that.

The burly, disfigured weapons master Gurney Halleck burst into the barracks, his voice booming commands. Flushed with anger, the beet-colored inkvine scar stood out like a lightning bolt on his face. "House shields are down! We're vulnerable!" Security teams had supposedly rooted out all the booby-traps, spy-eyes, and assassination devices left behind by the hated Harkonnen predecessors. Now the lumpish Halleck became a frenzy of barked orders.

Explosions sounded outside, shaking the barracks and rattling armor-plaz windows. Enemy assault 'thopters swooped in over the Shield Wall, probably coming from a Harkonnen base in the city of Carthag.

"Prepare your weapons!" Halleck bellowed. The buzzing of lasguns played across the stone walls of Arrakeen, incinerating buildings. Orange eruptions shattered plaz windows, decapitated observation towers. "We must defend House Atreides."

"For the Duke!" Uncle Hoh cried.

Elto yanked on the sleeve of his black uniform, tugging the trim into place, adjusting the red Atreides hawk crest and red cap of the corps. Everyone else had already jammed feet into boots, slapped charge packs into lasgun rifles. Elto scrambled to catch up, his mind awhirl. His uncle had pulled strings to get him assigned here as part of the elite corps. The other men were lean and whipcord strong, the finest hand-picked Atreides troops. He didn't *belong* with them.

Young Elto had been excited to leave Caladan for Arrakis, so far away. He had never ridden on a Guild Heighliner before, had never been close to a mutated Navigator who could fold space with his mind. Before leaving his ocean home, Elto had spent only a few months watching the men train, eating with them, sleeping in the barracks, listening to their colorful, bawdy tales of great past battles and duties performed in the service of the Atreides dukes.

Elto had never felt in danger on Caladan, but after only a short time on Arrakis, all the men had grown grim and uneasy. There had been unsettling rumors and suspicious events. Earlier that night, as the troops had bunked down, they'd been agitated, but unwilling to speak of it, either because of their commander's sharp orders or because the soldiers didn't know enough details. Or maybe they were just giving Elto, the untried and unproven new comrade, a cold shoulder ....

Because of the circumstances of his recruitment, a few men of the elite corps hadn't taken to Elto. Instead, they'd openly grumbled about his amateur skills, wondering why Duke Leto had permitted such a novice to join them. A signalman and communications specialist named Forrie Scovich, pretending to be friendly, had filled the boy with false information as an ill-conceived joke. Uncle Hoh had put a stop to that, for with his Jongleur's talent for the quick, whispered story—always told without witnesses because of the ancient prohibition—he could have given any of the men terrible nightmares for weeks ... and they all knew it.

The men in the Atreides elite corps feared and respected their supply sergeant, but even the most accommodating of them gave his nephew no preferential treatment. Anyone could see that Elto Vitt was not one of them, not one of their rough-and-tumble, hard fighting breed ....

By the time the Atreides house guard rushed out of the barracks, they were naked to aerial attack, from the lack of house shields. The men knew the vulnerability couldn't possibly be from a mere equipment failure, not after what they'd been hearing, what they'd been feeling. How could Duke Leto Atreides, with all of his proven abilities, have permitted this to happen?

Enraged, Gurney Halleck grumbled loudly, "Aye, we have a traitor in our midst."

Illuminated in floodlights, Harkonnen troops in blue uniforms swarmed over the compound. More enemy transports disgorged assault teams.

Elto held his lasgun rifle, trying to remember the drills and training sessions. Someday, if he survived, his uncle would compose a vivid story about this battle, conjuring up images of smoke, sounds, and fires, as well as Atreides valor and loyalty to the Duke.

Atreides soldiers raced through the streets, dodging explosions, fighting hard to defend. Lasguns sliced vivid blue arcs across the night. The elite corps joined the fray, howling—but Elto could already see they were vastly outnumbered by this massive surprise assault. Without shields, Arrakeen had already been struck a mortal blow.

✧ ✧ ✧

Elto blinked his eyes in the cave, saw light. A flicker of hope dissipated as he realized it was only a recharged glowglobe floating in the air over his head. Not daylight.

Still trapped in their tomb of rock, the Atreides soldiers listened to the continued thuds of artillery. Dust and debris trickled from the shuddering ceiling. Elto tried to keep his spirits high, but knew House Atreides must have fallen by now.

His uncle sat nearby, staring into space. A long red scratch jagged across one cheek.

During brief inspection drills while settling in, Elto had met the other important men in Duke Leto's security staff besides Gurney Halleck, especially the renowned Swordmaster Duncan Idaho and the old Mentat assassin Thufir Hawat. The black-haired Duke inspired such loyalty in his men, exuded such supreme confidence, that Elto had never imagined this mighty man could fall.

One of the security experts had been trapped here with the rest of the detachment. Now Scovich confronted him, his voice gruff and challenging. "How did the house shields get shut off? It must have been a traitor, someone you overlooked." The distrans bats seemed agitated in their cages at Scovich's waist.

"We spared no effort checking the palace," the man said, more tired than defensive. "There were dozens of traps, mechanical and human. When the hunter-seeker almost killed Master Paul, Thufir Hawat offered his resignation, but the Duke refused to accept it."

"Well, you didn't find all the traps," Scovich groused, probing for an excuse to fight. "You were supposed to keep the Harkonnens out."

Sergeant Hoh Vitt stepped between the two men before they could come to blows. "We can't afford to be at each other's throats. We need to work together to get out of this."

But Elto saw on the faces of the men that they all knew otherwise: they would never get out of the death trap.

The unit's muscular battlefield engineer, Avram Fultz, paced about in the faint light, using a jury-rigged instrument to measure the thickness of rock and dirt around them. "Three meters of solid stone." He turned toward the fallen boulders that had covered the cave entrance. "Down to two and a half here, but it's dangerously unstable."

"If we went out the front, we'd run headlong into Harkonnen shelling anyway," the gunner Deegan said. His voice trembled with tension, like a too-tight baliset string about to break.

Uncle Hoh activated a second glowglobe, which floated in the air behind him as he went to a bend in the tunnel. "If I remember the arrangement of the tunnels, on the other side of this wall there's a supply cache. Food, medical supplies … water."

Fultz ran his scanner over the thick stone. Elto, unable to move on his makeshift bed and fuzzed with painkillers, stared at the process, realizing how much it reminded him of Caladan fishermen using depth sounders in the reef fishing grounds.

"You picked a good, secure spot for those supplies, Sergeant," Fultz said. "Four meters of solid rock. The cave-ins have cut us off."

Deegan, his voice edged with hysteria, groaned. "That food and water might as well be in the Imperial Palace on Kaitain. This place … Arrakis … isn't right for us Atreides!"

The gunner was right, Elto thought. Atreides soldiers were tough, but like fish out of water in this hostile environment.

"I was never comfortable here," Deegan wailed.

"So who asked you to be *comfortable?*" Fultz snapped, setting aside his apparatus. "You're a soldier, not a pampered prince."

Deegan's raw emotions turned his words into a rant. "I wish the Duke had never accepted Shaddam's offer to come here. He must have known it was a trap! We can never live in a place like this!" He stood up, making exaggerated, scarecrowish gestures.

"We need water, the ocean," Elto said, overcoming pain to lift his voice. "Does anybody else remember *rain?*"

"I do," Deegan said, his voice a pitiful whine.

Elto thought of his first view of the sweeping wastelands of open desert beyond the Shield Wall. His initial impression had been nostalgic, already homesick. The undulating panorama of sand dunes had been so similar to the even patterns of waves on the sea … but without any drop of water.

Issuing a strange cry, Deegan rushed to the nearest wall and clawed at the stone, kicking and trying to dig his way out with bare hands. He tore his nails and pounded with his fists, leaving bloody patterns on the unforgiving rock, until two of the other soldiers dragged him away and wrestled him to the ground. One man, a hand-to-hand combat specialist who had trained at the famous Swordmaster school on Ginaz, ripped open one of their remaining medpaks and dosed Deegan with a strong sedative.

The pounding artillery continued. *Won't they ever stop?* He felt an odd, pain-wracked sensation that he might be sealed in this hell-hole for eternity, trapped in a blip of time from which there was no escape. Then he heard his uncle's voice ….

Kneeling beside the claustrophobic gunner, Uncle Hoh leaned close, whispering, "Listen. Let me tell you a story." It was a private tale intended only for Deegan's ears, though the intensity in the Jongleur's voice seemed to shimmer in the thick air. Elto caught a few words about a sleeping princess, a hidden and magical city, a lost hero from the Butlerian Jihad who would slumber in oblivion until he rose again to save the Imperium. By the time Hoh Vitt completed his tale, Deegan had fallen into a stupor.

Elto suspected what his uncle had done, that he had disregarded the ancient prohibition against using the forbidden powers of planet Jongleur, ancestral home of the Vitt family. In the low light

115

their gazes met, and Uncle Hoh's eyes were bright and fearful. As he'd been conditioned to do since childhood, Elto tried not to think about it, for he too was a Vitt.

Instead, he visualized the events that had occurred only hours before ....

✧ ✧ ✧

On the streets of Arrakeen, some of the Harkonnen soldiers had been fighting in an odd manner. The Atreides elite corps had shouldered lasguns to lay down suppressing fire. The buzzing weapons had filled the air with crackling power, contrasted with much more primal noises of screams and the percussive explosions of old-fashioned artillery fire.

The battle-scarred weapons master ran at the vanguard, bellowing in a strong voice that was rich and accustomed to command. "Watch yourselves—and don't underestimate *them*." Halleck lowered his voice, growling; Elto wouldn't have heard the words if he hadn't been running close to the commander. "They're in formations like Sardaukar."

Elto shuddered at the thought of the Emperor's crack terror troops, said to be invincible. *Have the Harkonnens learned Sardaukar methods?* It was confusing.

Sergeant Hoh Vitt grabbed his nephew's shoulder and turned him to join another running detachment. Everyone seemed more astonished by the unexpected and primitive mortar bombardment than by the strafing attacks of the assault 'thopters.

"Why would they use artillery, Uncle?" Elto shouted. He still hadn't fired a single shot from his lasgun. "Those weapons haven't been used effectively for centuries." Though the young recruit might not be well-practiced in battle maneuvers, he had at least read his military history.

"Harkonnen devils," Hoh Vitt said. "Always scheming, always coming up with some trick. Damn them!"

One entire wing of the Arrakeen palace glowed orange, consumed by inner flames. Elto hoped the Atreides family had gotten away .... Duke Leto, Lady Jessica, young Paul. He could still see their faces, their proud but not unkind manners; he could still hear their voices.

As the street battle continued, blue-uniformed Harkonnen invaders ran across an intersection, and Halleck's men roared in challenge. Impulsively, Elto fired his own weapon at the massed enemies, and the air shimmered with a crisscross web of blue-white lines. He fumbled, firing the lasgun again.

Scovich snapped at him. "Point that damn thing away from me! You're supposed to hit *Harkonnens*!" Without a word, Uncle Hoh grasped Elto's rifle, placed the young man's hands in proper positions, reset the calibration, then slapped him on the back. Elto fired again, and hit a blue-uniformed invader.

Agonized cries of injured men throbbed around him, mingled with frantic calls of medics and squad leaders. Above it all, the weapons master yelled orders and curses through twisted lips. Gurney Halleck already looked defeated, as if he had personally betrayed his Duke. He had escaped from a Harkonnen slave pit years before, had lived with smugglers on Salusa Secundus, and had sworn revenge on his enemies. Now, though, the troubadour warrior could not salvage the situation.

Under attack, Halleck waved his hands to command the entire detachment. "Sergeant Vitt, take men into the Shield Wall tunnels and guard our supply storehouses. Secure defensive positions and lay down a suppressing fire to take out those artillery weapons."

Never doubting that his orders would be obeyed, Halleck turned to the remainder of his elite corps, reassessing the strategic situation. Elto saw that the weapons master had picked his best fighters to remain with him. In his heart, Elto had known at that moment, as he did now thinking back on it, that if this were ever to be told as one of his uncle's vivid stories, the tale would be cast as a tragedy.

In the heat of battle Sergeant Hoh Vitt had shouted for them to trot double-time up the cliffside road. His detachment had taken their weapons and left the walls of Arrakeen. Glowglobes and portable illuminators showed firefly chains of other civilian evacuees trying to find safety in the mountainous barrier.

Panting, refusing to slacken their pace, they had gained altitude, and Elto looked down on the burning garrison city. The

Harkonnens wanted the desert planet back, and they wanted to eradicate House Atreides. The blood-feud between the two noble families dated all the way back to the Butlerian Jihad.

Sergeant Vitt reached a camouflaged opening and entered his code to allow them access. Down below, the gunfire continued. An assault 'thopter swooped along the side of the mountain, sketching black streaks of slagged rock; Scovich, Fultz, and Deegan opened fire, but the 'thopter retreated—after marking their position.

As the rest of the detachment raced inside the caves, Elto took a moment at the threshold to note the nearest artillery weapons. He saw five of the huge, old-style guns pounding indiscriminately at Arrakeen—the Harkonnens didn't care how much damage they caused. Then two of the mighty barrels rotated to face the Shield Wall. Flames belched out, followed by far-off thunder, and explosive shells rained down upon the cave openings.

"Get inside!" Sergeant Vitt shouted. The others moved to obey, but Elto remained fixated. In a single stroke, a long line of fleeing civilians vanished from the cliffside paths, as if a cosmic artist with a giant paintbrush had decided to erase his work. The artillery guns continued to fire and fire, and soon centered on the position of the soldiers.

The range of Elto's full-power lasgun was at least as far as the conventional shells. He aimed and fired, pulsing out an unbroken stream but expecting little in the way of results. But the dissipating heat struck the old-fashioned explosives in the loaded artillery shells, and the ragged detonation ripped out the breech of the mammoth cannon.

He turned around, grinning, trying to shout his triumph to his uncle—then a shell from the second massive gun struck squarely above the entrance to the cave. The explosion knocked Elto farther into the tunnel as tons of rock showered down, striking him. The avalanche sent shock waves through an entire section of the Shield Wall. The entire contingent was sealed inside ....

✿ ✿ ✿

After days in the tomblike cave, one of the glowglobes gave out and could not be recharged; the remaining two managed only a flickering light in the main room. Elto lay wounded, tended by the junior medic and his dwindling supplies of medicinals. Elto's pain had dulled from the broken glass to a cold, cold blackness that seemed easier to endure … but how he longed for a sip of water!

Uncle Hoh shared his concern, but was unable to do anything else.

Squatting on the stone floor off to his left, two sullen soldiers had used their fingertips to trace a grid in the dust; with light and dark stones they played a makeshift game of Go, a carryover from ancient Terra.

Everyone waited and waited—not for rescue, but for the serenity of death, for escape.

The shelling outside had finally stopped. Elto knew with a sick certainty that the Atreides had lost. Gurney Halleck and his elite corps would be dead by now, the Duke and his family either killed or captured; none of the loyal Atreides soldiers dared to hope that Leto or Paul or Jessica had escaped.

The signalman Scovich paced the perimeter, peering into darkened cracks and crumbling walls. Finally, after carefully imprinting a distress message into the voice patterns of his captive distrans bats, he released them. The small creatures circled the dusty enclosure, seeking a way out. Their high-pitched cries echoed from the porous stone as they searched for any tiny niche. After frantic flapping and swooping, at last the pair disappeared through a fissure in the ceiling.

"We'll see if this works," Scovich said. His voice held little optimism.

In a weak but valiant voice, Elto called his uncle nearer. Using most of his remaining strength, he propped himself on an elbow. "Tell me a story, about the good times we had on our fishing trips."

Hoh Vitt's eyes brightened, but for only a second before fear set in. He spoke slowly. "On Caladan …. Yes, the old days."

"Not so long ago, Uncle."

"Oh, but it seems like it."

"You're right," Elto said. He and Hoh Vitt had taken a coracle along the shore, past the lush pundi rice paddies and out into open water, beyond the seaweed colonies. They had spent days anchored in the foamy breakwaters of dark coral reefs, where they dove for shells, using small knives to pry free the flammable nodules called coral gems. In those magical waters they caught fan-fish—one of the great delicacies of the Imperium—and ate them raw.

"Caladan ..." the gunner Deegan said groggily, as he emerged from his stupor. "Remember how *vast* the ocean was? It seemed to cover the whole world."

Hoh Vitt had always been so good at telling stories, supernaturally good. He could make the most outrageous things real for his listeners. Friends or family made a game of throwing an idea at Hoh, and he would make up a story using it. Blood mixed with melange ... a great Heighliner race across uncharted foldspace ... the wrist-wrestling championship of the universe, between two dwarf sisters who were the finalists ... a talking slig.

"No, no stories now, Elto," the sergeant said in a fearful voice. "Rest now."

"You're a Master Jongleur, aren't you? You always said so."

"I don't talk about that much." Hoh Vitt turned away.

His ancestral family had once been proud members of an ancient school of storytelling on the planet Jongleur. Men and women from that world used to be the primary troubadours of the Imperium; they traveled between royal houses, telling stories and singing songs to entertain the great families. But House Jongleur fell into disgrace when a number of the itinerant storytellers were proven to be double agents in inter-House feuds, and no one trusted them any longer. When the nobles dropped their services, House Jongleur forfeited its status in the Landsraad, losing its fortunes. Guild Heighliners stopped going to their planet; the buildings and infrastructure, once highly advanced, fell into disrepair. Largely due to the Jongleur's demise, many entertainment innovations were developed, including holo projections, filmbooks, and shigawire recorders.

"*Now* is the time, Uncle. Take me back to Caladan. I don't want to be here."

"I can't do that, boy," he responded in a sad voice. "We're all stuck here."

"Make me *think* I'm there, like only you can do. I don't want to die in this hellish place."

With a piercing squeak, the two distrans bats returned. Confused and frustrated, they fluttered around the chamber while Scovich tried to recapture them. Even they had been unable to escape ....

Though the trapped men had held out little hope, the failure of the bats still made them groan in dismay. Uncle Hoh looked at them, then down at Elto as his expression hardened into grim determination.

"Quiet! All of you." He knelt beside his injured nephew. Hoh's eyes became glazed with tears ... or something more. "The boy needs to hear what I have to say."

✧ ✧ ✧

Elto lay back, letting his eyes fall half-closed as he readied himself for the words that would paint memory pictures on the insides of his eyelids. Sergeant Vitt sat rigid, taking deep breaths to compose himself, to center his uncanny skill and stoke the fires of imagination. To tell the type of story these men needed, a Master Jongleur must calm himself; he moved his hands and fingers in the ancient way, going through the motions he'd been taught by generations of storytellers, ritualistic preparations to make the story good and pure.

Fultz and Scovich shifted uneasily, and then moved closer, anxious to listen as well. Hoh Vitt looked at them with glazed eyes, barely seeing them, but his voice carried a gruff warning. "There is danger."

"Danger?" Fultz laughed and raised his grimy hands to the dim ceiling and surrounding rock walls. "Tell us something we don't know."

"Very well." Hoh was deeply saddened, wishing he hadn't pulled strings to get Elto assigned to the prestigious corps. The young man still thought of himself as an outsider, but ironically—by staying in the line of fire and destroying one of the artillery weapons—he had shown more courage than any of the proven soldiers.

Now Hoh Vitt felt a tremendous sense of impending loss. This wonderful young man, filled not only with his own hopes and dreams but also with those of his parents and uncle, was going to die without ever achieving his bright promise. He looked around, at the faces of the other soldiers, and seeing how they looked at him with such anticipation and admiration, he felt a moment of pride.

✧ ✧ ✧

In the hinterlands of Jongleur, a hilly rural region where Hoh Vitt had grown up, dwelled a special type of storyteller. Even the natives suspected these "Master Jongleurs" of sorcery and dangerous ways. They could spin stories like deadly spiderwebs, and in order to protect their secrets, they allowed themselves to be shunned, hiding behind a cloak of mystique.

"Hurry, Uncle," Elto said, his voice quiet and thready.

With intensity in his words, Sergeant Vitt leaned closer. "You remember how my stories always start, don't you?" He touched the young man's pulse.

"You warn us not to believe too deeply, to always remember that it's only a story ... or it could be dangerous. We could lose our minds."

"I'm saying that again to you, boy." He scanned the close-pressed faces around him. "And to everyone listening."

Scovich made a scoffing noise, but the others remained silent and intent. Perhaps they thought his warning was only part of the storytelling process, part of an illusion a Master Jongleur needed to create.

After a moment's hush, Hoh employed the enhanced memorization techniques of the Jongleurs, a method of transferring large amounts of information and retaining it for future generations. In this manner he brought to mind the planet Caladan, summoning it in every intricate detail.

"I used to have a wingboat," he said with a gentle smile, and then he began to describe sailing on the seas of Caladan. He used his voice like a paintbrush, selecting words carefully, like pigments precisely mixed by an artist. He spoke to Elto, but his story spread hypnotically, wrapping around the circle of listeners like the wispy smoke of a fire.

"You and your father went with me on weeklong fishing trips. Oh, those days! Up at sunrise and casting nets until sunset, with the golden tone of the sun framing each day. I must say we enjoyed our time alone on the water even more than the fish we caught. The companionship, the adventures and hilarious mishaps."

And hidden in his words were subliminal signals: *Smell the salt water, the iodine of drying seaweed …. Hear the whisper of waves, the splash of a distant fish too large to bring aboard whole.*

"At night, when we sat at anchor alone in the middle of the seaweed islands, we'd stay up late, the three of us, playing a fast game of tri-chess on a board made of flatpearls and abalone shells. The pieces themselves were carved from the translucent ivory tusks of South Caladan walruses. Do you remember?"

"Yes, Uncle. I remember."

All the men murmured their agreement; the Jongleur's haunting words were as real to them as to the young man who had actually experienced the memories.

Listen to the hypnotic, throbbing songs of unseen murmons hiding in a fog bank that ripples across the calm waters.

The shroud of pain grew fuzzy around Elto, and he could feel himself going to that other place and time, being carried away from this hellish place. The parched, dusty air at first smelled dank, then cool and moist. As he closed his eyes, he could sense the loving touch of Caladan breezes on his cheek. He smelled the mists of his native world, spring rain on his face, sea waves lapping at his feet as he stood on the rocky beach below the Atreides castle.

"When you were young, you would splash in the water, laughing and swimming naked with your friends. Do you remember?"

"I …" And Elto felt his voice merge with the others, becoming one with them. "We remember," the men mumbled reverently. All around them the air had grown close and stifling, most of the oxygen used up. Another one of the glowglobes died. But the men didn't know this. They were anesthetized from their pain.

See the wingboat cruising like a razorfin under dazzling sunlight, then through a warm squall under cloudy skies.

"I used to body surf in the waves," Elto said with a faint smile of wonder.

Fultz coughed, then added his own reminiscences. "I spent a summer on a small farm overlooking the sea, where we harvested paradan melons. Have you ever had one fresh out of the water? Sweetest fruit in the universe."

Even Deegan, still somewhat dazed, leaned forward. "I saw an elecran once, late at night and far away—oh, they're rare, but they do exist. It's more than just a sailor's story. Looked like an electrical storm on the water, but alive. Luckily, the monster never came close." Though the gunner had been hysterical not long before, his words held such an awed solemnity that no one thought to disbelieve him.

Swim through the water, feel its caress on your body. Imagine being totally wet, immersed in the sea. The waves surround you, holding and protecting you like a mother's arms ....

The two distrans bats, still loose from the signalman's cages, had clung to the ceiling for hours, but now they swayed and dropped to the floor. All the air was disappearing in their tomb.

Elto remembered the old days in Cala City, the stories his uncle used to tell to an entranced audience of his family. At several points in each of those tales, Uncle Hoh would force himself to break away. He had always taken great care to remind his listeners that it was *only a story*.

This time, however, Hoh Vitt took no breaks.

Realizing this, Elto felt a moment of fear, like a dreamer unable to awaken from a nightmare. But then he allowed himself to succumb. Though he could barely breathe, he forced himself to say, "I'm going into the water ... I'm diving ... I'm going deeper ..."

Then all the trapped soldiers could hear the waves, smell the water, and remember the whisper of Caladan seas ....

The whisper became a roar.

◇ ◇ ◇

In the velvet shadows of a crisp night on Dune, Fremen scavengers dropped over the ridge of the Shield Wall, into the rubble. Stillsuits softened their silhouettes, allowing them to vanish like beetles into crevices.

Below, most of the fires in Arrakeen had been put out, but the damage remained untended. The new Harkonnen rulers had returned to their traditional seat of government in Carthag; they would leave the scarred Atreides city as a blackened wound for a few months … as a reminder to the people.

The feud between House Atreides and House Harkonnen meant nothing to the Fremen—the noble families were all unwelcome interlopers on their sacred desert planet, which the Fremen had claimed as their own thousands of years earlier, after the Wandering. For millennia these people had carried the wisdom of their ancestors, including an ancient Terran saying about each cloud having a silver lining. The Fremen would use the bloodshed of these royal houses to their own advantage: the deathstills back at the sietch would drink deeply from the casualties of war.

Harkonnen patrols swept the area, but the soldiers cared little for the bands of furtive Fremen, pursuing and killing them only out of sport rather than in a focused program of genocide. The Harkonnens paid no heed to the Atreides trapped in the Shield Wall either, thinking none of them could have survived; so they left the bodies trapped in the rubble.

From the Fremen perspective, the Harkonnens did not value their resources.

Working together, using bare callused hands and metal digging tools, the scavengers began their excavation, opening a narrow tunnel between the rocks. Only a few dim glowglobes hovered close to the diggers, providing faint light.

Through soundings and careful observations on the night of the attack, the Fremen knew where the victims would be. They had uncovered a dozen already, as well as a precious cache of supplies, but now they were after something much more valuable, the tomb of an entire detachment of Atreides soldiers. The desert men toiled for hours, sweating into the absorbent layers of their stillsuits, taking only a few sipped drops of recovered moisture. Many water rings would be earned for the moisture recovered from these corpses, making these Fremen scavengers wealthy.

When they broke into the cave enclosure, though, they stepped into a clammy stone coffin filled with the redolence of death. Some

125

of the Fremen cried out or muttered superstitious prayers to Shai-Hulud, but others probed forward, increasing the light from the glowglobes now that they were out of sight of the nighttime patrols.

The Atreides soldiers all lay dead together, as if struck down in a strange suicide ceremony. One man sat in the center of their group, and when the Fremen leader moved him, his body fell to one side and a gush of water spewed out of his mouth. The Fremen tasted it. Salt water.

The scavengers backed away, even more frightened now.

Carefully, two young men inspected the bodies, finding that the uniforms of the Atreides were warm and wet, stinking of mildew and damp rot. Their dead eyes were open wide and staring, but with contentment instead of the expected horror, as if they had shared a religious experience. All of the dead Atreides soldiers had clammy skin ... and something even more peculiar, revealed when the Fremen cut them open.

The lungs of these dead men were entirely filled with water.

The Fremen fled, leaving their spoils behind, and resealed the cave. Thereafter, it became a forbidden place of legend, drawing wonder from anyone hearing the story as it was passed on by Fremen from generation to generation.

Somehow, sealed inside a lightless cave in the driest desert, all of the Atreides soldiers had *drowned* ....

After the Scattering

Sea Child

Introduction

"Sea Child" takes place during the events of Frank Herbert's last Dune novel, *Chapterhouse Dune*. The beleaguered Bene Gesserit Sisterhood face their destructive dark counterparts, the Honored Matres, who have destroyed the planet Dune.

This story was written to help raise money for the Tsunami Relief anthology *Elemental*. It provides an introduction to the chronological grand finale to the Dune series, *Hunters of Dune* and *Sandworms of Dune*, based on Frank Herbert's last "Dune 7" outline.

Sea Child

Bene Gesserit punishments must carry an inescapable lesson, one which extends far beyond the pain.

— Mother Superior Taraza, Chapterhouse Archives

As she had done since the brutal Honored Matres conquered Buzzell, Sister Corysta struggled to get through the day without attracting undue notice. Most of the Bene Gesserit like herself had already been slaughtered, and passive cooperation was the only way she could survive.

Even for a disgraced Reverend Mother such as herself, submission to a powerful though morally inferior adversary galled her. But the handful of surviving Sisters here on the isolated ocean world— all of whom had been sent here to face years of penance—could not hope to resist the "whores" that arrived unexpectedly, in such overwhelming force.

At first, the Honored Matre conquerors had resorted to primal techniques of coercion and manipulation. They killed most of the Reverend Mothers during interrogation, trying unsuccessfully to learn the location of Chapterhouse, the hidden homeworld of the Bene Gesserits. Thus far, Corysta was one of twenty Sisters who had avoided death, but she knew their odds of continued survival were not good.

Back in the terrible Famine Times after the death of Leto II, the God Emperor of Dune, much of humanity had scattered into the wilderness of star systems and struggled to survive. Left behind in the core of the old Imperium, only a few remnants had clung to the tattered civilization and rebuilt it under Bene Gesserit rule. Now, after fifteen hundred years, many of the Scattered Ones were coming back, bringing destruction with them. At the head of the unruly hordes, Honored Matres swept across planets like a raging spacestorm, returning with stolen technology and grossly altered attitudes. In appearance, the whores bore superficial similarities to the black-robed Bene Gesserits, but in reality they were unimaginably different, with different fighting skills and no apparent moral code—as they had proved many times with their captives on Buzzell.

As dawn gathered light across the water, Corysta went barefoot to a jagged inlet, finding precarious balance on slippery rocks as she made her way down to the ocean's edge. The Honored Matres kept the bulk of the food supplies for themselves, offering little to the surviving inhabitants of Buzzell. Thus, if Corysta failed to find her own food, she would starve. It would amuse the whores to find out that one of the hated Bene Gesserits could not care for herself; the Sisterhood had always taught the importance of human adaptation for survival in challenging environments.

The young Sister had a knot in her stomach, pangs of hunger similar to the pains of grief and emptiness. Corysta could never forget the crime that had sent her to Buzzell, a foolish and failed effort to keep her baby secret from the Sisterhood and their interminable breeding program.

In moments of despair, Corysta felt she had two sets of enemies, her own Sisters and the Honored Matres who sought supremacy over everything in the old Imperium. If the Bene Gesserits did not find a way to fight back—here and on other planets—their days would be numbered. With superior weaponry and vast armies, the Honored Matres would exterminate the Sisterhood. From her own position of disadvantage, Corysta could only hope her Mother Superior was developing a plan on Chapterhouse that would enable the ancient organization to survive. The Sisterhood faced an immense challenge against an irrational enemy.

In a fit of violence, the Honored Matres had been provoked into unleashing incredible weapons from the Scattering against

Rakis, the desert world better known as Dune. Now, that planet was nothing more than a charred ball, with all sandworms dead and the source of spice obliterated. Only the Bene Gesserits, on faraway Chapterhouse, had any stockpiles left. The whores from the Scattering had destroyed tremendous wealth simply to vent their rage. It made no sense. Or did it?

Soostones were also a source of wealth in the Known Universe, and they were found only on Buzzell. Therefore, the Honored Matres had conquered this planet with its handful of punished Bene Gesserit Sisters. And now they meant to exploit it ….

At the water's edge, Corysta reached into the lapping surf, withdrawing her handwoven traps that gathered night-scurrying crustaceans. Lifting her skirt, she waded deeper to retrieve the nets. Her special little cove had always provided a bounty of food that she shared with her few remaining Sisters.

She found footing on the slick surface of a submerged rock. The moving currents stirred up silt, making the water murky. The sky was steel gray with clouds, but she hardly noticed them. Since the arrival of the Honored Matres, Corysta spent most of her time with her gaze lowered, seeing only the ground. She'd had enough punishment from the Bene Gesserit. As unfair as it was in the first place, her suffering had been exacerbated by the whores.

As she pulled in the net she had laid at sunset, Corysta was pleased to feel its heaviness, which indicated a good catch. *Another day without starvation.* With difficulty she dragged the net closer to the rocks—and discovered that its tangled strands held not a clatter of shellfish but, instead, a weak and greenish creature. A small humanoid baby with smooth skin, large round eyes, a wide mouth, and gill slits. She recognized the creature as one of the genetically modified "phibian" slaves the whores had brought to Buzzell for harvesting soostones. It was just an infant, floating alone and helpless.

Catching her breath, Corysta splashed back to the shore rocks behind her. Phibians were cruel and monstrous—no surprise, considering the vicious whores who had created them—and she was afraid she would be beaten for interfering with this abandoned child. Adult phibians would accuse her of catching the infant in her nets, claim that *she* had killed it. She had to be very careful.

Then Corysta saw the baby's eyes flutter open, its gills and mouth gasping for oxygen. A bloody gash marred the infant's forehead; it looked like an intentional mark drawn by the single claw of a larger phibian. This child was weak and sickly, with a large discoloration on its back and side, a glaring birthmark like ink spilled on its small body.

An outcast.

She had heard of this before. Among the phibians, the claw wound was a mark of rejection. Some aquatic parent had scarred its own frail child in disgust because of the birthmark, and then cast the baby away to perish in the seas. Stray currents had brought it to Corysta's nets.

Gently, she untangled the creature and washed the small, weak body in the pool. It was male. Responding to her ministrations, the sickly phibian stirred and opened its alien, membranous eyes to look at her. Despite the monstrous appearance, Corysta thought she saw humanity behind the strange eyes, a child from the sea who had done nothing to deserve the punishment inflicted upon it.

She gathered the baby in her arms, folding him in her black robe to hide him from view. Looking around, Corysta quickly ran home.

✧ ✧ ✧

Buzzell's deep, plankton-rich oceans swallowed all but a few patches of rough land. It was as if the cosmic creator had accidentally left a water tap running and filled the planet to overflowing.

On the only patch of dry land suitable for use as a spaceport, Corysta worked with several other beaten Bene Gesserit Sisters. The women carried heavy sealed boxes of the milky soostones. After all their specialized training, including a remarkable ability to control their bodily chemistry, Corysta and these defeated Sisters were nothing more than menial laborers forced to work while the brutal Honored Matres flaunted their dominance.

Two Bene Gesserit women walked beside Corysta with their eyes cast down, each one carrying a heavy satchel full of the harvested gems. The Honored Matres enjoyed grinding the disgraced Reverend Mothers under their heels. During their exile here, Corysta and her fellow Sisters had all known everyone's crimes and support- ed one another regardless. But in their current situation, such minor infractions and the irrelevant penance and retribution meant noth- ing. She and her companions knew the impatient whores were sure to kill them soon, rendering their life histories meaningless. Now that the phibians had arrived as a specialized workforce, the Sisters were no longer necessary for the economic processes of Buzzell.

On Corysta's left, five adult phibians rose out of the water, lean and powerful forms with frightening countenances. Their unscaled skins shone with oily iridescence; their heads were bullet-shaped, streamlined for swimming. The Honored Matres had apparent- ly bred the creatures using technology and knowledge brought by Tleilaxu gene masters who had also fled in the Scattering. Exper- imenting with human raw materials, had those Tleilaxu outcasts cooperated willingly, or had they been forced by the whores? The sleek and glistening phibians had been well designed for their un- derwater work.

The humanoids stood dripping on the land, carrying nets full of gleaming soostones. Corysta no longer found the jewels ap- pealing. To her, they had the look and smell of the blood that had been spilled to get them. Thousands of Buzzell inhabitants—exiled Sisters, support personnel, even smugglers and traders—had been slaughtered by the Honored Matres in their takeover.

The whores in charge of the work crew snapped orders, and Corysta took a webbed net from the first phibian. On the creature she smelled salty moisture, an iodine-laced body odor, and an undertone of fish. The slitted eyes were covered by a moist nictitating membrane.

Looking at the repugnant face, she sensed coldness, and won- dered if this might be the father of her sea child, who was now se- cretly recovering in her hut. As that thought crossed her mind, the adult phibian struck a blow that knocked her backward. In a bubbly voice, the creature said, "Too slow. Go work."

She grabbed the satchel of soostones and scurried away. She did not want the Honored Matres to focus on her. Her instinct for survival was ever-present.

No one would be coming to rescue them. Since the devas- tation of Rakis, the Bene Gesserit leadership had holed up on

Chapterhouse to hide from the unrelenting hunters. She wondered if Taraza was still Mother Superior of the order, or if—as rumor suggested—the Honored Matres had killed her on Rakis.

On this backwater world, Corysta and her companions would never know.

✧ ✧ ✧

That evening, in her hut lit by a glowing fish-oil lamp, Corysta cradled the phibian baby in her arms and fed it broth with a spoon. How ironic that her own child had been taken from her by the Breeding Mistresses, and now in a strange cosmic turnabout she had been given this ... creature. It seemed a cruel joke played by Fate, a monster in exchange for her beautiful baby.

Immediately she chastised herself for thinking that way. This poor subhuman child had no control over its surroundings, its parentage, or the fate that had befallen it.

She held the moist, cool baby close in the dim light and could feel the strange humming energy of its body next to hers, almost a purring sensation that made no detectable sound. At first the baby had fussed about the spoon, refusing to eat from it, but gradually, patiently, Corysta coaxed it to accept the thin broth boiled with crustaceans and seaweed. The baby hardly ever whimpered, though it looked at her with the saddest expression she'd ever seen.

Life was so unpredictable, moment by moment and year by year, and so chaotic within the much larger chaos of the entire universe. People were anxious to do this and that, to go in directions they imagined were important.

As Corysta gazed down at the phibian and made gentle eye contact with it, she had the sensation of supreme balance, that the time they were spending together had a healing influence on the frenzied cosmos ... that all of the chaos wasn't really what it appeared to be, that her actions and experiences had a larger, significant purpose. Each mother and child extended far beyond their own parochial circumstances, far beyond the horizons they could see or even begin to imagine.

In the distant past, the Bene Gesserit breeding program had focused on creating a genetic foundation that would result in the Kwisatz Haderach, supposedly a powerful unifying force. For thousands of years the Sisterhood had sought that goal, and there had been many failures, many disappointments. Worse, when they finally achieved success with Paul Atreides, Muad'dib, the Kwisatz Haderach had turned against them and torn apart their plan. And then his son, Leto II, the Tyrant—

"Never again!" the Bene Gesserit had vowed. They would never try to breed another Kwisatz Haderach, and yet their careful sifting and twining of bloodlines had continued for millennia. They must be trying for something. There must have been some reason her own baby had been torn from her.

Corysta had been ordered by Breeding Mistress Monaya to obtain specific genetic lines that the Sisterhood claimed it needed. She had not been told where she fit into the larger picture; that was an unnecessary complication in the eyes of her superiors. Complete information was known only to a select few, and orders were passed on down the ranks to the frontline soldiers.

I was one of those soldiers. Corysta had been commanded to seduce a nobleman and bear his child; she was instructed to feel no love for him or for the baby. Against her natural, inborn instincts she was supposed to shut off her emotions and perform the task. She was no more than a vessel carrying genetic material forward, eventually turning over the contents to the Sisterhood. Just a container of sperm and ovum, germinating something her superiors needed.

Inadvertently she had won half the battle; she hadn't cared at all about the man. Oh, he'd been handsome enough, but his spoiled and petulant personality had soured her even as she seduced him. She had gone away without ever telling him that she carried his child.

But the other half of the battle that came later was far more difficult. After carrying the baby for nine months, nourishing it from her own body, Corysta knew she would be unable to turn it over to Monaya. Shortly before her due date, she had sneaked away into seclusion, where all alone she gave birth to a daughter.

Only hours into the baby's life, before Corysta had time to know her own child, Sisters stormed in like a flock of angry black crows. Stern-faced Monaya took the newborn herself and spirited her away to be used for their secret purposes. Still weak from giving birth, Corysta knew she would never see her daughter again, that she could never call it her own. Despite all she tried to feel for the girl child, the baby daughter had never belonged to her, and she'd only been able to steal moments with it. Even her womb was not her own.

Of course Corysta had been foolish in running, in trying to keep the baby for herself. Her punishment, as expected, had been severe. She'd been exiled to Buzzell, where other Sisters in her situation were sent, all of them guilty of crimes of love that the Sisterhood could not tolerate … "crimes of humanity."

How peculiar to label love a crime. The universe would have disintegrated long ago without love, shattered by immense wars. To Corysta, it seemed inhuman for Bene Gesserit leadership to take such a position. The Sisters were, in their own way, compassionate, caring people, but Reverend Mothers and Breeding Mistresses spoke of "love" only in derogatory or clinical terms.

The Sisterhood reveled in defying compartmentalization, in espousing an odd juxtaposition of beliefs. Despite their apparent inhumanity in running roughshod over desires of the heart, the Sisters considered themselves expert at key aspects of being human. Similarly, the indoctrinated women professed to have no religion, but behaved as if they did anyways, adopting a strong moral and ethical base and rituals that could only be classified as religious.

Thus the complex, enigmatic Sisters were simultaneously human and inhuman, loving and unloving, secular and religious … an ancient society that operated within its narrow rules and belief systems, walking tightropes they had suspended over deep chasms.

To her misfortune, Corysta had fallen off one of the tightropes, plunging her into darkness.

And in her punishment, she had been sent here to Buzzell. To this strange sea child …

✧ ✧ ✧

As a storm whipped across the waters, ruffling the sea into whitecaps, Honored Matres dragged the surviving Bene Gesserits in front of the commandeered administrative buildings. The damp wind felt bitter on Corysta's face as she stood on an expanse of grass that was growing too long, since no one tended it. She dared to lift her chin, her own small act of defiance.

The Honored Matres were lean and wolfish, their faces sharp, their eyes feral orange from the adrenaline-based spice substitute they consumed. Their bodies were all sinew and reflexes, their hands and feet edged with hard calluses that could be as deadly as any weapon. The whores wore clinging garments over their figures, bright leotards and capes adorned with fine stitching. They flaunted themselves like peacocks, used sex to dominate and enslave the male populations on worlds they conquered.

"So few of you witches remain," said Matre Skira as she stood before the assembled Sisters. "So few …" The sharp-featured leader of the whores of Buzzell, she had long nails, compact breasts like clenched fists, and knotted limbs with all the softness of petrified wood. She was of an indeterminate age; Corysta detected subtle behavioral hints that Skira believed that everyone thought she was much younger than she actually was. "How many more of you must we torture before someone reveals what we need to know?" Her voice carried an artificial undertone of honey, yet it burned like acid.

Jaena, the Sister standing next to Corysta, blurted, "All of us. No Bene Gesserit will ever tell you where Chapterhouse is."

Without warning, the Honored Matre struck out with a powerful kick of her leg, flashing like a whip. Before Jaena could even draw back, the hard side of Skira's bare foot danced across the outspoken Sister's forehead with a blur of speed.

"Trying to provoke me into killing you?" Skira asked in a surprising calm voice, after she landed back with the perfect balance and grace of a ballerina.

Skira had displayed precise control, delivering a blow just sufficient to cut the skin on Jaena's forehead. She left a bloody gash that looked remarkably similar to the mark of rejection on Corysta's sea child.

The injured Sister dropped, clutching her forehead. Blood streamed between her fingers, while her attacker chuckled. "Your stubbornness amuses us. Even if you don't provide us with the information we desire, you are at least a source of entertainment." Other Honored Matres laughed with her.

After returning from the Scattering, legions of whores used economics, military weapons, and sexual bondage against the human populations they encountered. They hunted the Bene Gesserits like prey, taking advantage of the Sisterhood's lack of strong political leadership or effective military forces. But still the Honored Matres feared them, knowing the Bene Gesserits remained capable of real resistance as long as their leadership remained in hiding.

As the storm continued to build out on the ocean, whipping wind and rain across the strip of land where the women stood, Matre Skira proceeded to question Jaena and two other Sisters, screaming at them and beating them … but keeping them alive.

Thus far, Corysta—ever quiet and alert as she shivered in the cold—had avoided the brunt of her captors' anger. In the past she'd been interrogated like the others, but not with the severity she had feared. Now the regular proceedings had evolved into light entertainment for the whores, who conducted them more out of habit than from any realistic hope of acquiring vital knowledge. But violence always simmered just beneath the surface, and the young Sister knew a massacre could occur at any moment.

The rain let up, and Corysta wiped moisture from her face. Despite the punishment and exile the Bene Gesserit had imposed, they remained loyal to the Sisterhood. She would kill herself before revealing the location of Chapterhouse.

Finally Skira and the other Honored Matres returned to the comfort and warmth of their administrative buildings. With a swirl of patterned capes over damp leotards, the whores left Corysta and her companions to make their way back through the rain to their squalid daily lives, supporting their wounded Sisters.

Hurrying along a cliffside trail that led to her hut after she had left the others, Corysta watched the surf crashing against rocks below and wondered if the phibians were looking up at her through the stippled waves. Did the amphibious creatures even think about the child they had marked and then abandoned to the sea? They must assume it to be dead.

Glad to have survived another interrogation, she ran home and slipped into her primitive dwelling where the baby waited, now healthier and stronger.

✿ ✿ ✿

Corysta knew she could not keep the phibian child forever.

Her moments of happiness were often ephemeral, like fleeting flashes of light in the gloom of a dark chamber. She had learned to accept the precious moments for what they were—just moments.

Though she wanted to clutch the sea child to her breast and keep it safe, she knew that was not possible. Corysta wasn't safe herself—how could she hope to keep a child safe? She could only protect the baby temporarily, giving him shelter until he grew strong enough to go off on his own. She would have to release him back into the sea. From the phibian child's rapid rate of growth, she felt certain that he would become self-sufficient faster than a human could.

One evening, Corysta did something she had dreaded. As darkness set in, she made her way down to her hidden cove along the familiar path, taking the child with her. Though she could not always see the way in the gloom, she was surprised at how sure-footed she was.

Wading out into the cold water, she cradled the child securely in her arms, and heard him whimper as the water touched his legs and lower body. She'd hidden and cared for her sea child for almost two months now, and already he was the size of a human toddler. His blotchy, prominent birthmark bothered her not at all, whether or not his own people had cast him out because of it. The terrifying prospect of this evening had been on her mind for weeks, and she'd feared that the phibian would just swim away and never look back at her. Corysta knew his connection with the ocean was inevitable.

"I'm here," she said in a gentle voice. "Do not be afraid."

With his webbed hands, the child clung to her arms, refusing to let go. The rapidly humming pulse of his skin against hers revealed the baby's silent terror.

Corysta waded back to the shallows, where the water was only a few inches deep, and sat there on the sand, letting the waves wash over her legs and the baby's. The water was warmer than the cool evening air, and felt good as it touched her. Out to sea, the water glowed faintly phosphorescent, so that the bullet-shaped head was profiled against the horizon. The darkness of the small shape reminded her of the mysteries contained within him, and in the ocean beyond …

Each evening thereafter, Corysta developed a routine. As darkness set in, she would go to her hidden cove and dip into the water, taking the tiny phibian along. Soon the creature she called Sea Child was walking alongside her and swimming in shallow water on his own.

Corysta wished she could be a phibian herself and swim out there, to the farthest reaches of this ocean world, escaping the brutal Honored Matres and taking her sea child with her. She wondered what it would be like to dive deep into the ocean, even if she did so on an unseen tether. At least there she might experience a familial hold that was stronger than anything she felt toward her Bene Gesserit Sisters.

◊ ◊ ◊

Corysta prodded Sea Child to speak, but the phibian succeeded only in making primitive sounds from an undeveloped larynx.

"I'm sorry I can't teach you properly," she said, looking down at the toddler as he played on the stone floor of her hut, moving on his webbed hands and feet. She was about to prepare breakfast, combining crustaceans with native herbs she had collected from between the rocks.

The child looked at her without apparent comprehension. He was surrounded by crude toys she had made for him, shells and woody kelp knobs on which she had marked smiling faces. Some of the faces were human, while others she'd made to look like Sea Child's own people. Curiously, he showed more interest in the ones that least resembled him.

The toddler stared into the carved human face on the largest piece of wood, picking it up with clumsy fingers. Then he looked up in sudden alarm, toward the door of the hut, peeling back his thick lips to expose tiny sharp teeth.

Corysta became aware of sounds outside and felt a bitter, sinking sensation. She barely had time to gather up the child and hold him against her before the door burst open in a hail of splinters.

Matre Skira loomed in the doorway. "What sort of witchery is this?"

"Stay away from us! Please."

Sinewy women in tight leotards and black capes surrounded her. One of them tore the phibian child from her grasp; another beat her to the floor in a flurry of fists and sharp kicks. At first Corysta tried to fight back, but her efforts were hopeless, and she covered her face. The blows still got through. One broke her nose, and another shattered her arm. She cried out in pain, knowing that was what the whores wanted, but her physical discomfort didn't compare with the terrible anguish she felt over losing a child. *Another* child.

Sea Child was hidden from her view, but she heard the baby phibian make his own terrible sounds, high-pitched squeals that chilled her to the bone. Were the Honored Matres hurting him? Anger surged through her, but she could not fight back against their numbers.

These whores from the Scattering—were they offshoots of the Bene Gesserit, descendants of Reverend Mothers who had fled into space centuries ago? They returned to the old Imperium like evil doppelgängers. And now, despite the dramatic differences between Honored Matres and Bene Gesserit, both groups had taken a child from Corysta.

She screamed in frustration and rage. "Don't hurt him! Please. I'll do anything, just let me keep him."

"How touching." Matre Skira rounded on her, feral eyes narrowing. "But do you mean it? You'll do anything? Very well, tell us the location of Chapterhouse, and we will let you keep the brat."

Corysta froze, and nausea welled up insider her. "I can't."

Sea Child let out a very human-sounding cry.

The Honored Matres scowled viciously. "Choose—Chapterhouse, or the child."

She couldn't! Or could she? She'd been trained as a Bene Gesserit, sworn her loyalty to the Sisterhood ... which had, in turn, punished her for a simple human emotion. They had exiled her here because she dared to feel love for a child, for her own child.

Sea Child was not like her, but he did not care about Corysta's shame, nor did she care about a patch of discoloration on his skin. He had clung to her, the only mother he had ever known.

But she was a Bene Gesserit. The Sisterhood ran through every cell of her body, through a succession of Other Lives descending through the endless chain of ancestors whom she had discovered upon becoming a Reverend Mother. Once a Bene Gesserit, always a Bene Gesserit ... even after what the Sisterhood had done to her. They had already taught her what to do with her emotions.

"I can't," she said again.

Skira sneered. "I knew you were too weak." She delivered a kick to the side of Corysta's head.

A black wave of darkness approached, but Corysta used her Bene Gesserit bodily control to maintain consciousness. Abruptly, she was jerked to her feet and dragged down to the cove, where the women threw her onto the spray-slick rocks.

Struggling to her knees, Corysta fought the pain of her injuries. To her horror she saw Skira wade into shallow water with Sea Child. The little phibian struggled against her and kept looking toward Corysta, crying out eerily for his mother.

Her own baby had not known her so well, snatched from her arms only hours after birth. Corysta had never gotten to know her own little daughter, never learned how the girl's life had been, what she had accomplished. Corysta had known this poor, inhuman baby much more closely. She had been a real mother, for just a little while.

Restrained by two strong women, Corysta saw froth in the sea just offshore, and presently she made out hundreds of swimming shapes in the water. *Phibians.* Half a dozen adults emerged from the ocean and approached Matre Skira, dripping water from their unclothed bodies.

Sea Child cried out again and reached back toward Corysta, but Skira held his arms and blocked his view with her own body.

Corysta watched helplessly as the adult phibians studied the mark of rejection on the struggling child's forehead. Would they just kill him now? Trying to remain strong, Corysta wailed when the phibians took her child with them and swam out to sea.

Would they cast him out again like a tainted chick from a nest, pecked to death and cast out? Corysta already longed to see him—if the phibians were going to kill him, and if the whores were going to murder her, she wanted at least to cling to him. Her Sea Child!

Instead, she saw a remarkable thing. The phibians who had originally rejected the child, who had made their bloody mark on the baby's forehead, were now clearly helping him to swim. Supporting him, taking him with them. They did not reject him!

Her vision hampered by tears, she saw the phibians disappear beneath the waves. "Goodbye, my darling," she said, with a final wave. She wondered if she would ever see him again … or if the whores would just break her neck with a swift blow now, leaving her body on the shore.

Matre Skira made a gesture, and the other Honored Matres released their hold, letting Corysta drop to the ground. The evil women looked at one another, thoroughly amused by her misery. They turned about and left her there.

She and Sea Child were still prisoners of the Honored Matres, but at least she had made the phibian stronger, and his people would raise him. He would prove the phibians wrong for ever marking him.

She had given him life after all, the true maternal gift. With a mother's love, Corysta hoped her little one would thrive in deep and uncertain waters.

Treasure in the Sand

Introduction

This tale takes place after the events in *Chapterhouse Dune,* after the vicious Honored Matres have turned the planet Dune into a seemingly lifeless charred ball, a place where only the most desperate searchers would go.

Treasure in the Sand

"When the last worm dies and the last melange is harvested upon our sands, these deep treasures will spring up throughout our universe. As the power of the spice monopoly fades and the hidden stockpiles make their mark, new powers will appear throughout our realm."

—Leto Atreides II, the God Emperor of Dune

Pressing his fingers against the windowport of the Spacing Guild landing shuttle, Lokar stared at the blasted world beneath them. Rakis, once called Dune—home of the holy sandworms, the only natural source of the spice melange, the place where the God Emperor Leto II had gone into the sand.

Now everything was dead, incinerated by the obliterating weapons of the Honored Matres ....

Lokar, one of the last Priests of the Divided God, closed his eyes before tears could come. *Giving water to the dead. To a whole dead world.* He murmured a prayer, which was drowned out by the sound of dry air currents that buffeted the descending ship.

"The planet looks like one giant scab. How can there be anything left down there?" asked Dak Pellenquin. Lokar didn't like him; he was the expedition member who had talked loudest and bragged most frequently during the Heighliner journey to Rakis. "One giant scab. Is this expedition going to be worth our while? Worth *anyone's* while?"

"We'll find whatever there is to find." Guriff, the expedition leader, cut him off. "Our priest will show us where to dig." Guriff had close-cropped dark hair, narrow-set eyes, and a persistent bristly stubble on his chin, no matter how often he attended to his facial hygiene. "Anything left down there—that whole planet is ours for the taking."

"Only because no one else wants it," said a stocky man. He had a jovial expression, but icy cold eyes behind his forced smile. This one called himself Ivex, though rumor held that this was not his true name. He propped his feet up on the empty seat in front of him.

Lokar didn't answer any of them, just clung to his prayer like a lifeline, eyes shut. Joining these treasure hunters on the departure planet of Cherodo had been a risk, but the devout priest had considered his options. Rakis was the most sacred of all worlds, home of the great sandworms that comprised the Divided God. Away from Rakis on a mission during the cataclysm, Lokar had survived by the purest luck—or divine destiny. He must recover what he could, if only to atone.

Since scanning had proved imprecise on the planet still in flux after the bombardment, Lokar had offered to use his own instincts and firsthand knowledge to guide their searches. Among many poor choices, this one made the most sense, the only way he could afford to travel back to what was left of his beloved Rakis. A last, desperate pilgrimage.

He had agreed to accompany their "archaeological expedition"—what a euphemism!—under very specific terms. CHOAM, the ancient and powerful trading organization, financed the expedition for its own reasons, hoping for a financial boon. They had agreed to the priest's demands, drawn up a contract, and specified the terms. Provided the Priest of the Divided God could indeed show the scavengers the way, Guriff's men were authorized to grab whatever physical treasures they managed to dig out of the blasted sands, but any sacred relics would be turned over to Lokar (though the distinction between "sacred relics" and "treasure" remained uncomfortably nebulous).

A slender woman stepped out of the cockpit and looked at the hodgepodge members of the expedition. Representing CHOAM,

Alaenor Ven had reddish-gold hair that hung to her shoulders, the strands so precisely neat and straight that they seemed held in place with a nullentropy field. Her eyes were crystalline blue, her facial features flawlessly (and probably artificially) sculpted to the absolute perfection one might find on the visage of a mannequin. In an odd way, her very lack of flaws made her seem cold and unattractive.

"CHOAM has provided all the equipment you will need. You have two survey 'thopters, two groundcars, prefabricated shelters, excavation machines, and supplies for two months. Even with all of the sand plankton killed, sample probes show the air is thin but breathable. The oxygen content remains tolerable, though diminished."

Ivex gave a scornful laugh. "How can that be? If sand plankton create the oxygen, and they were all burned away—"

"I merely report the readings. I do not explain them. You will have to find your own answers."

Listening without participating, Lokar nodded quietly to himself at the obvious explanation: It was a miracle. There had always been mysteries about the planet Dune. This was just one more.

"Though the environment is not as inhospitable as one might expect, do not allow yourselves to be overconfident. Rakis is still a harsh place." She looked at them again. "We land in forty minutes. Our schedule permits you only three standard hours to unload and make your preparations."

Eleven members of the team shifted in their seats, fully attentive; two pretended to sleep, as if ignoring the challenges they would face; the remaining three peered through the windowports with varying levels of interest and trepidation.

Pellenquin cried, "Three hours? Can't you wait a day or two to make sure we're not stranded there?"

Guriff scowled at his own crewman. "The Spacing Guild has schedules and customers. If you don't trust your own survival abilities, Dak, you have no business on my team. Tear up your contract now and go back with Alaenor Ven if you like."

"I would if she'd have me," Ivex said with a snort. A few others chuckled in their seats. The icily beautiful CHOAM woman's expression did not change at all.

High overhead, the huge Heighliner that had carried them here orbited the seared desert planet as the landing shuttle set down on the unmarked ground. Devastating weapons had entirely reshaped the terrain—cities leveled, mountains turned to glass, oceans of sand vitrified. A few sketchy landmarks remained, and despite the planet's unpredictable magnetics, the transport's deep-scan probes had found enough of a street grid to identify the buried city of Keen. The team would set up camp there.

When the cargo doors opened onto the glassy, baked plain, Guriff's team wore oxygen intensifiers with supplemental tanks on their shoulders. Lokar was the first to remove his breather and inhale deeply. The air was thin and dry, with what others found to be an unpleasant burnt smell; even so, when he filled his lungs, the taste was sweet. He was returning home. He fell to his knees on the hard, scorched sand, thanking the Divided God for bringing him back safely, for helping him to continue holy work.

Guriff went over to the kneeling priest and nudged him roughly. "Work now, pray later. You'll have plenty of time to commune with your desert once we set up the camp."

Under a tight schedule, the crew threw themselves into the task at hand. Guriff shouted orders to them, and the scavengers moved about unloading the groundcars and 'thopters, removing the shelter structures, prefabricated huts, crates of food supplies, and large barrels of water. To protect the exploratory 'thopters and groundcars, they erected a hangar dome.

For his own shelter, Lokar had specified a simple desert tent. To really understand this planet, to touch its pulse, the Holy Books of the Divided God said it was better to live on the surface and in natural rock formations, facing the heat, sandstorms, and behemoth worms. But this was not the old Rakis, not a great planetary expanse of windblown sand. Much of the loose sand had turned to glass, and surely the great worms had all perished in the conflagration. The scavengers spoke excitedly of the great treasure the God Emperor was said to have concealed on Rakis. Though no one had found the hoards in thousands of years, during prime conditions on Rakis, the scavengers hoped the very devastation had churned something up from the depths.

In less than three standard hours, they had unloaded the equipment and supplies. All the while, the CHOAM representative stood staring at the wasteland, frequently consulting her wrist-embedded chronometer. She stepped back into the transport precisely when her schedule told her to do so. "A ship will return to gather whatever you have found in thirty standard days. Complete your survey and assess any value this planet retains." Her voice became harder. "But do not disappoint us."

With a hum of suspensor engines and a roar of displaced air, the large landing shuttle climbed back into the atmosphere, leaving Lokar with Guriff's crew, alone on an entire planet.

✧ ✧ ✧

Like frenzied worker bees, the treasure hunters laid out their equipment and gear, ready to begin their work. Guriff and his men fanned out with handheld probes, using several models of Ixian ground-penetrating scanners in a useless attempt to peer through the sandy surface. Lokar watched them with patient skepticism. The Divided God would never make their work so simple. They would have to labor, sweat, and suffer for any gains they achieved.

These men would learn, he knew.

It was late afternoon, with the sun low in the restless atmosphere, but the men were anxious to get underway, frustrated by the long wait of the journey. They made a lot of noise, unlike the old days when such vibrations would have brought the monster worms. Not anymore. Lokar felt a wave of sadness.

Off by himself, he moved to a low spot, a glassy featureless depression that he thought might be the center of the lost city. He placed himself in relation to the low rocky escarpments that distinguished the site from the rest of the bleak surroundings. The sensation felt right, as if his entire life and all its experiences, large and small, had pointed him in this direction.

The Priests of the Divided God had placed many of the God Emperor's treasures in safekeeping at their temple in the city of Keen. Though he held only a middle rank, Lokar had once seen the protected subterranean vaults. Perhaps those chambers were far enough beneath the surface to have survived the bombardment.

The air, while dry and thin, was disturbingly cool, as if the planet's great furnace had flickered out. But he could not shake the belief that his Divided God still lived here, somehow. As he stared, hypnotically drawn to the shimmering and melted surface, Lokar began to see with a different set of eyes.

He walked around the blasted city with an increasing sensation. Each step of the way he knew exactly where he was. When he narrowed his eyes, ancient structures began to appear around him like mirages, dancing on the sand in ghostly, flickering color, as if his mind had its own scanner.

Am I going mad? Or am I receiving divine guidance?

A few hundred meters away, the others gathered around the expedition leader, shaking their heads at their equipment in anger, hurling it to the ground and cursing it. Pellenquin shouted, "Just like they said. Our damned scanners don't work here!"

Although Guriff brought out a tough, thin map printed on spice paper, he and his companions could not get their bearings. Annoyed, he stuffed it back in his pocket.

"Maybe our priest will have a revelation," Ivex said with a forced chuckle.

Guriff led them over to Lokar. "Priest, you had better earn your keep."

Still seeing spectral images of the lost city, he nodded distractedly. "The Divided God is speaking to you through this planet. All of your technology didn't destroy it. Rakis still has a pulse."

"*We* didn't destroy it," Pellenquin protested. "Don't blame us for this."

"Mankind is a single organism. We are all responsible for what occurred here."

"He's talking strangely," Ivex said. "Again."

"If you insist on thinking that way, you will never understand." Lokar narrowed his eyes, and the illusory splendor of the great city danced beyond and around the men. "Tomorrow, I will show you the way."

❖ ❖ ❖

As he slept alone in his flimsy tent, listening to the rustle of silence outside, Lokar lived through a peculiar dream. He saw the Temple at Keen restored in all of its glory, with dark-robed priests going about their business as if the Divided God would last forever.

Lokar had not been one of the Priesthood's elite, though he'd undergone rituals and tests that could one day grant him entry into the most secret sanctums. In his dream he gazed through the slit-window of a tower that overlooked the sands, the realm of the holy worms. A procession of hooded priests entered the tower room and gathered around him. They pulled down their hoods to reveal their faces: Guriff, Pellenquin, Ivex, and the others.

The shock awoke him, and he sat up in the darkness of his tent. Poking his head out through the flap seals, Lokar smelled moisture in the darkness, an oddly heavy nightscent unlike any of the Rakian odors he remembered. What had the bombardment done to the cycles of water on this planet? In bygone days there had been sub-terranean caches of water, but the devastating weapons must have damaged them, broken them loose. He drew another deep breath, savoring the smell. Moist air on Rakis!

Above the disconcertingly bumpy eastern horizon, the sky glowed softly red, then brightened with sunrise to profile the nubby, melted escarpments. The treasure hunters emerged from their stiff-walled shelters and milled around.

Lokar walked out onto the sandy surface. The men formed a circle outside, opened food and beverage packages provided by CHOAM, and made faces as they chewed and swallowed. He picked up a breakfast pack and joined them, lifting a self-heating coffee cup from an extruded holder on his plate. The dark blend should have had melange in it, especially on Rakis. It had been so long since he'd had good spice coffee.

Eager to get started, stocky Ivex tested his handheld scanner again. In disgust he tossed it into a half-buried storage bin.

At sunset the night before, their two survey 'thopters had already taken off for a first look at the surrounding area. When they returned, the men had streamed out of them like enraged bees. Lokar didn't have to hear their complaints and expectations. Their faces told it all. Rakis had not met their expectations, and now they were stuck here for at least a month.

Guriff said, "We're relying on you, Priest. Where is the buried temple?" He pointed over his left shoulder. "That way?"

"No. Government offices were in that direction, and the Bene Gesserit keep."

The expedition leader brought out the rumpled spice-paper map. "So the temple was more to the west?"

"Your map is flawed. Important streets and structures are missing. The scale is off."

"Reliable documents about Rakis are hard to come by, especially now. No one thought maps of Keen would ever be useful again."

"I'm your only reliable map now." He could easily have led them off track, but he was anxious to explore the religious site himself—and they had the appropriate tools. "Remember, according to my CHOAM agreement, I am to be the caretaker of the most important religious artifacts. And I am to decide which artifacts are the most significant."

"Yes, yes." Guriff's eyes flashed angrily. "But first you have to find something for us to discuss."

Lokar pointed to the northwest. "The great Temple of Keen is that way. Follow me."

As if his comment had fired the starting gun in a race, the scavengers ran for digging machines kept in the 'thopters and began assembling the components. He had seen the powerful wheeled machines demonstrated back on Cherodo, during preparation for the expedition.

As the priest led the treasure hunters across the desolate sand, he hoped he was doing the right thing. *If God didn't want me to do this, he would tell me so.* With each step, a more intense trancelike state came over him, as if the Divided God were still transmitting across the cosmos, telling the priest exactly what to do, despite the grievous injury that had been committed against Him.

Through narrowed eyes, Lokar absorbed the images of the lost buildings, and the grandeur of Keen danced around him. These unbelievers noticed nothing more than dead rolling sand around them. He led the men along a thoroughfare that only he could see, a wide boulevard that once had been lined with devout followers. Behind him, the men chattered anxiously over the soft rumble of their rolling, self-propelled digging machines.

At the main entrance of the Temple, where a statue-lined bridge had once crossed a deep, dry arroyo, Lokar pointed a wavering finger downward. "Dig there. Carefully."

Two men donned protective suits and climbed onto a pair of digging machines. Side by side, they began to bore downward at an angle into the fused sandy surface, blasting a reinforced shell into the soft, sloping walls. Behind them, the exhaust funnels spewed dirt back out with great force, shooting material high into the air.

Guriff handed an imager headset to the priest. "Here, watch the progress of the drilling. Tell us if you see anything wrong."

When Lokar put the device on, the illusory images of the city faded in his mind, leaving only ugly reality. He watched as the tunnelers reached a glassy-black surface several meters beneath the surface—the remains of a melted structure that had been covered over by blowing sand. The headlamps of the digging machines revealed a partially uncovered door and an ancient symbol.

He transmitted an urgent signal to the tunnelers, halting their machines. "They've reached the entrance to one of the meeting chambers!" He and Guriff climbed down the fused slope into the deep hole, pressing past the tunnelers. "Remove the door carefully."

One of the men activated a small, spinning drill on his machine, while the other tunneler produced a mechanical hand that held several small, black cartridges. While Lokar and Guriff looked on, the men drilled holes in the door and inserted cartridges. Before the priest could express his alarm, tiny explosions went off, and the ancient, heavy door shuddered and tilted, and a narrow opening showed on the hinge side. The men used a hook to pull the door open, then shone a bright light inside the chamber.

A partially collapsed ceiling hung like a thunderhead over a room filled with debris. Lokar squeezed through the opening and entered the room, demanding the right of first inspection. He hunched beneath a section of partially collapsed ceiling, scuttled across the rough floor.

"The whole thing could cave in on you," Guriff warned. Lokar knew, though, that the Divided God would not allow that, not after all he'd been through.

His heart beating wildly, he spotted a glittering object in the pile of debris and shoved rubble aside to clear a large platinum-colored goblet capped with an engraved lid so that the symbolic blood of God would not evaporate into the dry desert air.

Digging deeper into the pile, he found something more interesting, a small golden statue of a sandworm rising out of the desert and turning its proud, eyeless face upward to the heavens. Excited, the priest set it next to the goblet.

Then, like a miracle, he noticed moisture seeping down a wall behind the debris pile. Could it be? What was the source? Hearing a rumble, he looked upward and saw the ceiling start to give way over his head. Water trickled and then poured on him—*water* on Rakis! Grabbing the goblet and the statuette, he ran for the doorway. Just as he squirmed out next to Guriff, the whole room collapsed behind him in a roar.

"What do you have there?" the expedition leader asked, looking at the goblet as if nothing remarkable had happened.

"This goblet should have some value to you. I believe it is made of rare metal." Lokar handed it to Guriff, while slipping the sandworm sculpture into the pocket of his wet robe. "This is something more sacred. Not for outside eyes."

With a shrug, Guriff said, "It's a start." He swung up the goblet's metal lid to investigate whether the large vessel contained any other treasure. He cried out as a tiny creature jumped out and scampered partway up the inclined tunnel, then stopped and looked back at the intruders with tiny, dark eyes.

"Damn thing bit me!" Guriff rubbed a red spot on his thumb. "How the hell did it survive?"

"It's just a mouse," one of the men said. "Something's alive here after all."

"A desert mouse. The ancient Fremen called it muad'dib," Lokar murmured in awe. "The mouse that jumps."

The two tunnelers left their machines and ran up the fused incline, boisterously chasing after the creature.

"Terrible catastrophe will befall anyone who harms a muad'dib," Lokar cried. The rodent easily scurried away from its pursuers and disappeared into a tiny opening in the doorway.

Guriff rolled his eyes. "Now you consider a *mouse* a sacred object?"

✧ ✧ ✧

Two weeks later, the sunset looked like a layer of spilled blood over a hot flame. Dust smeared the horizon in an ominous approaching line. The air around the settlement, which normally held a silence so deep as to be a hole of sound, was alive with an angry background hum like buried thunder.

Lokar knew what the signs meant. Because of his human failings, he felt the thrill of fear; because of his religious faith, he felt awe. Rakis was wounded, perhaps mortally, but not entirely dead. The planet was restless in its sleep.

"What I wouldn't give for a set of weathersats." Guriff propped his hands on his hips and sniffed the air. "That looks dangerous." He had already called back the exploration 'thopters and groundcars, though a team continued to dig in the tunnels of buried Keen, excavating a large labyrinth underground.

"You know what it is," Lokar said. "You can see. It's a storm, maybe the mother of them all."

"I thought that with the bombardment, with the fusing of so much sand, the usual Coriolis Effect—"

"This will not be usual, Guriff. Not in any way." The priest continued to stare. He had not moved. "The whole environment has been thrown into turmoil. Some weather patterns might have been suppressed, and others inflamed." Lokar nodded toward the blood-red horizon. "We will be lucky if we survive this night."

Taking the warning seriously, Guriff shouted for his men, picked up a commlink and summoned his teams for an immediate emergency meeting. "Tell me then, Priest, what shall we do? You've lived through storms here before. What is our best option for shelter? In the tunnels under Keen, or sealed inside our shelters? What about the hangar dome? Will the vehicles be safe?"

Lokar responded with a vacant smile and a shrug. "I shall remain in my tent, but you do whatever you see fit. Only God can save us. No shelter in the universe can protect you if He deems that tonight is the night you will die."

Guriff cursed under his breath, then trudged off to meet with his crew ….

That night the wind howled like an awakening beast, and abrasive sand scratched against the fabric of the priest's small tent. The storm whispered and muttered maddening temptations like the hoarse voice of Shaitan.

Lokar huddled with his bony knees drawn up to his chest, his arms wrapped around them, his eyes closed. He recited his prayers over and over, raising his voice until he was practically shouting against the roar outside. The true God could hear even the tiniest whisper, no matter what the background din might be, but Lokar comforted himself by hearing his own words.

The reinforced tent fabric stretched taut, as if demons were breathing against it. Lokar knew he could survive this storm. A storm had unquestionable power—yet faith was more powerful still.

Lokar held on, rocking himself throughout the night. He heard a clatter and a groan as one of the camp's larger, heavily armored structures was torn apart in the gale, but if he ran outside, the blowing sand grains would flay the flesh from his bones.

The men of Guriff's team had made their choices and placed their bets. Some had dug themselves underground in Keen; others believed in the security of their own structures. Their fates had been written by a hand of fire in the Book of Heaven from the moment they were born. In the morning after the storm had passed, Lokar would see what had been decided.

Hours passed, and he didn't actually sleep so much as go into a deep trance. Sand and dust sprinkled his face, caking his eyes and his nose.

Finally, he blinked and looked around him to see washed-out daylight. Miraculously, his tent still stood erect, but the fabric had been scoured down to fine gauzy remnants. Breezes, now gentle in the exhausted aftermath of the terrific winds, spilled through tiny gaps in the tent, stirring against him. The priest stood up and parted the spiderweb-thin fibers of the wall of his tent, like a man emerging from a womb.

Rakis seemed pristine and virginal. He blinked into the dawn radiance, rubbed the dust from his face, and stared at the freshly scoured landscape. The early morning sunlight sparkled across fresh sand that had been freed from the glassy crust that covered so many dunes.

Debris from the entire encampment had scattered, probably over an expanse of kilometers. Nearby, one of the prefabricated structures had been destroyed, and everyone inside was surely dead. Although the hangar dome was also breached, the vehicles and 'thopters were still intact, though damaged.

Lokar heard shouts and voices, other members of the scavenging team crawling out of where they had huddled during the night, assessing the losses, counting the casualties, and cursing. Guriff's voice was unmistakable as he shouted profanities, finding one set of wreckage after another.

Lokar couldn't believe he had survived in his tiny shelter, where he should have been wiped out. There was no logical explanation, but a Priest of the Divided God did not look for logic. He found himself wrapped up in his own revelation, his own ecstasy. He bent down to the fresh sand at his feet, scooped up a handful and looked at it in his palm. He pinched a single grain between thumb and forefinger and lifted it to the sunlight, studying the sparkle. He saw in even this tiny fleck of silica a symbol of miraculous, divine power. He smiled.

Without warning, Guriff slapped his hand, and cuffed Lokar in the side of the head. The priest blinked and turned to the expedition leader, whose face was red with anger and disgust. Guriff had lost so much during the night that he needed to take out his outrage on someone.

Lokar refused to be rattled. "Be thankful, Guriff. You survived."

Disheartened, the man stalked away. A few moments later, Lokar went to join him, offering his assistance. God had saved them for a reason.

The robed priest stood on a high lump of rock, gazing across the mottled, lifeless wasteland. The lens of dust in the air made the rising orange sun appear larger than normal.

Like immense birds riding the air currents, the two repaired ornithopters approached from the night, flying low over the desert, flapping their wings rhythmically. In the week following the storm, disgusted with the lack of success at Keen, Guriff had sent his scouts to search the south polar regions for treasure sites. Optimistically and unrealistically, the scavengers hoped they might find signs of ancient hidden vaults exposed by the upheaval. Lokar knew they would find nothing. The Divided God would reveal his treasure only to the faithful—like himself.

Lokar climbed down from the rock and made his way across the makeshift field as the aircraft landed. Guriff came forward to meet the 'thopter crews and receive his report.

The rough-and-tumble scout leader knocked dust from his clothes. "Nothing down south at all. We landed more than twenty times and poked around, took core samples, tested the deep scanners." He shook his head. "Looks like Keen is all we have."

In the background, the priest heard engines whirring to life, the drone of tunneling machines as they awoke for the day. Excavation crews had so far discovered a handful of artifacts, a sealed chest of clothes, flatware, broken pieces of furniture, portions of tapestries, a few relatively undamaged statues.

"Even junk collectors wouldn't pay more than ten solaris for these scraps," Pellenquin had said in disgust.

The priest did not share the general feeling of disappointment. Something valuable would turn up, if they persisted in their efforts. But God had his own tricks, and perhaps Guriff and his crew would not see the treasure in front of their eyes.

As the returning scouts from the second 'thopter plodded toward the settlement to curl up and sleep in the heat of the day, the tunnel-riddled ground trembled. On the other side of the camp, a cloud of dust spurted upward, accompanied by a loud thud and shouts. Guriff and the men ran toward the excavations. "Cave-in!"

Within the hour, all working together, they pulled two bodies out of the dirt. Lokar recognized a pair of young men who had been eager to contribute, anxious to earn their fortunes. Guriff bitterly watched the bodies being wrapped for chemical cremation. The team was still reeling from the damage the unexpected storm had inflicted. "There is treasure on Rakis," Lokar said, trying to reassure him. "We just have to look in the right place."

"You're as blind as your precious worms, Priest!"

"The worms of Rakis were never blind. They simply saw in a different manner."

"They didn't see the obliteration of their planet coming," Guriff said, and Lokar had no response.

Gazing out at the barren, blasted planet, Lokar turned and strode out onto the wasteland. Though he took no water or supplies, he walked for hours as the day warmed and the air began to shimmer. He ventured farther from camp than he had ever gone before.

Out on the sand, instinctively Lokar walked with an irregular shuffling step in the manner of the Fremen who used to live here, as if any worms still existed deep underground that might be able to detect him. He felt something driving him forward, galvanizing his energies, enticing him.

Far from view of the camp, with only a trail of footprints snaking behind him to show him the way back, Lokar climbed up a wide, gnarled rock formation under the harsh afternoon sunlight. He reached the top and gazed across the expanse. Something dark and rounded caught his eye, an obstruction large enough to form a stark lip of shadow. It seemed to call to him.

Lokar made his way down the other side of the rock and plodded across the desert. The sinuous mound was larger than it looked, as if most of it was still covered by the sand. Its exterior was mottled and weathered with splotches of black, like a giant buried tree trunk. He touched it and pulled back as sand and dust sloughed down from a rough, pebbly surface. Lokar fell to his knees in the dust.

A sandworm had risen to the surface and perished in the last shocks of the bombardment of Rakis, roasted alive. These weathered cartilaginous remnants had been burned, fused with a layer of glassy sand, exposed by the shifting storms.

In the loose sand that had gathered in the lee of the obstruction, he discovered a fist-sized ball of clear glass, perfectly spherical.

Filled with wonder, Lokar dug it out, then found another melted sphere buried beside it. These nodules of flash-melted sand were not an unusual consequence of the ferocious heat of the attack. But placed where they were, beneath the head of the fallen worm, Lokar interpreted them as something entirely different. *The tears of God.* Out on the blasted landscape, staring in wonder at the hulk of the long-dead worm, Lokar felt a new kind of light suffusing him from all directions. Just as he had seen ghostly visions of the lost city of Keen, he now also saw the entire planet as it once had been, in all of its perilous glory. No matter what the Honored Matres had done, all the splendor of Rakis was not gone. The treasure was everywhere, for all of the faithful. The priest knew exactly what the Divided God wanted him to do.

Lokar smiled beatifically. "We just weren't looking for it with the proper eyes."

✿ ✿ ✿

The CHOAM ship returned in a month, exactly on schedule. Exploring at random in the ruins of Keen and the collapsed Temple, Guriff ordered his prospectors to continue their scavenging and excavation work up to the last minute, hoping to find some lost treasure to justify the expedition.

The expedition leader had managed to consolidate what remained of his crew, but two days ago the useless priest had gone missing. Guriff had sent an ornithopter out to search for the frustrating man, but gave up the effort after a few hours. Lokar was mad; they should never have wasted time or supplies on him in the first place. But the trading company had hired him, sent him along.

As soon as the large CHOAM transport ship landed, workers emerged from the transport, scurrying about like ants on the sand. They opened the cargo doors and removed equipment.

Guriff was surprised to see the priest disembark onto the blasted sands with the coldly beautiful Alaenor Ven. How had they gotten together? The cargo shuttle must have found him wandering like a lunatic on the sands. Guriff didn't know why they would have bothered to rescue the man.

As he watched Lokar and the woman talking, not even looking in his direction, the expedition leader balled his fists. He was tempted to stride over and knock down the babbling priest for being so reckless, not acting as part of this crew. But he realized that his outburst would be childish, and he doubted the cool, businesslike representative would have the time or patience for power plays like that. Instead, Guriff decided it would be better for him to ignore the situation entirely, retreat to his headquarters hut, and put together documents and records. *She* could come to *him*. He sealed the door against oxygen and moisture loss and made himself a cup of potent spice coffee using the last scraps of melange from their supplies.

As he sat in his sealed chamber, Guriff listened to the hum of excavating machines outside, the groan of equipment. New diggers? He didn't know what the company was doing out there, nor could he understand why Alaenor Ven continued to ignore him. Did she not want her report?

At last she unsealed the door and strode into his headquarters hut without signaling or asking permission. She probably thought she owned the entire camp because CHOAM had supplied it.

Not letting her take control of the conversation, Guriff faced her clear blue eyes. "My team and I would like to stay for another month. We have not found the wealth you expected, but I'm convinced that the legends of the God Emperor's treasure hoards are true." He had no direct evidence to support what he said, but he would not give up. Not yet.

She responded with a thin smile. "Oh, the treasure is here all right—more wealth than we can imagine, perhaps more than CHOAM could sell."

"Then I'll find it," Guriff said. "We'll keep digging, keep hunting."

"Perhaps you will find something else of interest, but my transport already has a hold full of treasure, something you overlooked. Quite foolishly, I must say. We found the priest Lokar out in the desert, and he convinced me that he had found something of great value. Priests are very good salesmen, you know."

Guriff felt his skin grow hot. "What has the crazy priest found? He reported nothing to me." He pushed past the woman, and she

165

slowly turned to watch him as he unsealed the door hatch and marched toward the landed transport.

Lokar stood there on the ramp, looking saintly. The last large pieces of equipment had been rolled back aboard. A great deal of digging had been done in the sand around the landing area.

Guriff grabbed him by the collar of his robes. He felt betrayed, after all his effort, all the disasters his misbegotten crew had faced. "What have you been hiding from me?"

"I have hidden nothing. It was right in front of you all the time."

"Explain yourself."

"I am a messenger of God, chosen to continue His great work. Even though the priesthood is mostly dead, even though our temples have been leveled here on Rakis, our belief remains widespread across the galaxy. Many new cults and spinoff sects have sprung up. The faithful continue to believe and worship. They need more. They need their Divided God."

"What does that have to do with treasure?"

Lokar slumped down onto the ship's ramp, sitting there as if meditating. Guriff wanted to strangle him.

"You simply don't understand, Guriff." The CHOAM woman walked calmly up to him. "Treasure and wealth are a matter of definitions. You defined your search too narrowly."

He walked up the ramp, ignoring her, demanding to see exactly what they had loaded into their hold. Guild and CHOAM workers had returned to their seats, preparing to take off again. Crates of new camp supplies had been left behind on the ground to be sorted and restacked by the scavenger crew. It was certainly enough to last them for another month. He would demand that the woman take Lokar with her when she departed.

Guriff pushed his way down the aisle with Alaenor Ven following him. He reached the back, where a hatch led into the cargo bay.

"You forgot to recognize the importance and power of religion," she said, continuing as if she had never paused. "Even if the fanatics are not wealthy, they will sacrifice everything to pay for something they believe is important. They truly revere their Divided God."

Guriff worked the hold's controls, but missed the proper button. He slapped his palm on the wall and rekeyed the pad. Finally, the hatch slid open.

The transport's cargo hold was full of sand.

Ordinary sand.

The CHOAM woman continued to smile. "The faithful seek any sort of artifact from Rakis. Sacred relics. Even in the best of times, only the richest and most dedicated could afford to make a pilgrimage to their sacred Dune. Now that the planet is dead and almost all travel cut off, every scrap—every holy artifact—is worth even more."

"You're planning to sell *sand?*"

"Yes. Beautiful in its simplicity, isn't it?"

"I've never heard of anything so absurd."

"CHOAM will file for the necessary mining rights and patents to prevent claim jumpers. When word gets out, of course, there will be smugglers and purveyors of fraudulent goods, but those are all problems we can deal with."

Lokar came up beside them and beamed as he stared into the dusty, sand-filled hold. Stepping forward, he bent down and thrust his hands into the soft grains, pulling up handfuls. "Isn't it wonderful? Offworld, throughout the Old Empire, even a tiny vial of this sand will sell for many solaris. People will line up for a single grain, to touch the dust to their lips."

"The sand must flow," the CHOAM woman said.

"You're all idiots." In disgust, Guriff exited the transport and went to meet what was left of his crew. They were pleased at the stacks of fresh supplies. When they asked him about the departing priest and what the CHOAM representative had said, he refused to answer, gruffly telling them to get back to work. They all had risked everything to come here, and they needed to find something worthwhile on Rakis. Something other than sand.

As the heavily laden transport ship lifted off, kicking up a blast of sand around it—*worthless sand*, in his view—Guriff looked at the barren landscape and imagined the real treasure out there, treasure that he would find.

About the Author

Brian Herbert is the author of multiple *New York Times* bestsellers. He has won a number of literary honors, including the *New York Times* Notable Book Award, and has been nominated for the highest awards in science fiction. After more than five years in development, he published *Dreamer of Dune*, a moving biography of his father (Frank Herbert) that was a Hugo Award finalist. His acclaimed novels include the *Timeweb* trilogy (*Timeweb*, *The Web and the Stars*, and *Webdancers*); *The Stolen Gospels*; *The Lost Apostles*; *The Race for God*; *Sidney's Comet*; *Sudanna, Sudanna*; and *Man of Two Worlds* (written with Frank Herbert).

Kevin J. Anderson has published 140 books, 56 of which have been national or international bestsellers. He has written numerous novels in the Star Wars, X-Files, and DC Comics universes, as well as unique steampunk fantasy novels *Clockwork Angels* and *Clockwork Lives*, written with legendary rock drummer Neil Peart, based on the concept album by the band Rush. His original works include the Saga of Seven Suns series, the Terra Incognita fantasy trilogy, the Saga of Shadows trilogy, and his humorous horror series featuring Dan Shamble, Zombie PI. He has edited numerous anthologies, written comics and games, and the lyrics to two rock CDs. Anderson and his wife Rebecca Moesta are the publishers of WordFire Press.

Together, Herbert and Anderson have written 18 books in the Dune series as well as their own epic science fiction trilogy, *Hellhole*, *Hellhole Awakening*, and *Hellhole Inferno*.

If you liked *Tales of Dune,* you might also enjoy:

by Kevin J. Anderson

Tau Ceti (with Steven Savile)
Tucker's Grove
Alternitech
Blindfold
Climbing Olympus
Clockwork Angels: The Comic Scripts
Resurrection, Inc.
The Saga of Seven Suns, Veiled Alliances
Hopscotch

Dan Shamble, Zombie PI Series
Dan Shamble 1: Death Warmed Over
Dan Shamble 2: Unnatural Acts
Dan Shamble 3: Hair Raising
Dan Shamble 4: Slimy Underbelly
Dan Shamble 5: Working Stiff

Gamearth Series
Gamearth 1: Gamearth
Gamearth 2: Gameplay
Gamearth 3: Game's End

Million Dollar Series
Million Dollar Productivity
Million Dollar Professionalism for the Writer
Worldbuilding: From Small Towns to Entire Universes

by Brian Herbert

The Race for God
The Stolen Gospels 1: The Stolen Gospels
The Stolen Gospels 2: The Lost Apostles

Memorymakers
  Marie Landis & Brian Herbert

Storm World
  Bruce Taylor & Brian Herbert